The Snow Man

Valerie Kershaw

Duckworth

First published in 1979 by
Gerald Duckworth & Co. Ltd.
The Old Piano Factory
43 Gloucester Crescent, London NW1

ISBN 0 7156 1421 5

Typeset by Computacomp (UK) Ltd
Fort William, Scotland
and printed by
Unwin Brothers Limited, Old Woking, Surrey

1

Of course, she had known it was going to be cold. When was that? This morning, at breakfast, she had seen beyond the angle of David's nose, beyond the blank gable end of a semi-detached, and become aware of an iced granite sky.

'Are you going back into work after you've been to the dentist?' He had folded the newspaper and picked up his coffee cup.

Should she tell him, she wondered. Was it too soon? She could, after all, be mistaken. Her fingers lightly touched her belly, as if somehow she could draw out the secrets of her body, know of them.

'No. I've got one or two days off still owing to me from last year. If I don't take them now I'll never get them.'

'Could you get my suit from the cleaners then?'

'All right.' Her gaze wandered back to the window. Small eddies of snow crystallised, glittering in darting sun, and then all was grey once more. She buttered some toast, but she was restless. She didn't eat it. 'Going to snow,' she said.

'That's what the weather forecast says.' He picked up his newspaper again.

Their eyes met suddenly across the breakfast table. They were laughing at each other.

'Snowballs,' he said. 'It's years since I was in a good snowball fight. God, is that the time?' He began to gulp his coffee.

Snowmen, she thought. We used coal for their buttons.

3

And marbles for their eyes. Those big marbles. Was it gobs? Gobbies? She couldn't remember. She felt in the pocket of her housecoat for her cigarettes. Again her fingers had touched her belly, quickly, bewilderedly.

There were small beginnings of panic in her: a panic that was now a raging anger. Her foot was hard down on the accelerator of the Volkswagen. The seat belt wasn't fastened. Impatiently she shook her long brown hair out of her eyes, and her gloved hand reached to turn on the windscreen wipers. The snow was shunted into arcs— iced granite—and discoloured with the yellow of petrified lava. That had been the breakfast sky. But now it was night. It was beginning to snow heavily, and the car was buffeted by a sniping wind.

The headlights made a swirling planet, a Saturn of elements. She couldn't see the mountain, she couldn't see Rake Top. But she could feel its presence. She didn't think about it, but put the engine into second gear and turned left up its flank.

Perhaps she ought to go back home. David said there would be ice on the road—shouted at her to stop being a bloody fool, to come back. The row which had precipitated her flight had flared up so suddenly. It had been over such a minor thing: the telephone bill. He'd opened up his mail in the evening when he came in from work.

'My God! What have you been doing? Phoning Australia?'

'No. Of course I haven't.'

'Jesus Christ. How could you run up a bill like this?'

'You use the phone too.'

'I don't gossip. I don't spend hours gossiping on the bloody thing. My God, you were on to Dora the other day ... natter, natter, natter. The woman only lives round the corner! Practically next door.'

'Oh, shut up. Shut up. Shut up!' she was yelling, her hands over her ears, tears springing into her eyes. She had almost knocked the hall-stand over as she grabbed her sheepskin coat. 'I won't hear any more. I can't take any more!' She ran out of the house, leaving David standing, uncomprehending, at the glass front door of their semi-detached.

What had she really been in such a fury about? The afternoon, she thought: the long, cold afternoon when Maureen had invited her over for coffee and some of the other women on the estate had congregated in her lounge-diner. It was a room like a corridor, really, and sometimes sleet drifted into the panes of the picture windows. The fish drifted too, glowing eerily in the tank by the television.

Dora, plump and Jewish, aggressively intent on her three-year-old daughter. 'Ride a cock horse to Banbury Cross ...'

Maureen, smoking, knitting, seizing an occasional chocolate from an opened box and demolishing it with her sharp teeth, telling the wives again: 'Of course, they turned Matthew three times. I was actually in labour before the head came down.'

'My waters broke when I was in the market,' Juliette observed briskly, adjusting her glasses. 'I was at the fish stall. I was in the queue. We were going to have fish for tea.'

And the children squealing and Maureen's indignant voice: 'Justin hit Matthew with that car!'

'Your Matthew took Justin's tractor,' Dora adjudicated and, bending to her own child: 'Little Bo-peep has lost her sheep ...' They were so close that they were woven together like threads of the same garment.

Maureen savoured her chocolate and stretched stringy legs. 'I keep getting this pain in my side. And I feel really rotten. My head is hammer, hammer, too. It was so bad that I went to bed at nine o'clock, but of course he still wanted his two penn'orth.'

'Our Nicola can count to four,' Dora announced.

5

'Come on, say it, Nicky. Do it. After mummy. One, two, three, four ... Come on, don't be silly.'

The room was so dark now that Christie said: 'It's more like night than afternoon.'

Nicola chimed 'One, two, three, four—' and three pairs of hostile, adult eyes found her out. She retreated deeper into receiving thighs. 'There. Who's my clever girl,' Dora crooned.

'I'm not being funny, but isn't it a little early to start teaching numbers? She's barely three.'

Dora either hadn't heard Maureen's remark or chose not to hear it. She turned her lips to her child's ear. 'One, two, buckle my shoe ... three, four, knock on the door ...'

'You put the kettle on,' Juliette told Christie. 'We'll keep an eye on the kids.'

'About time you got started, Christie, you know,' Maureen observed. 'How long have you been married now? Two years, isn't it?'

Christie hadn't answered. She got up and threaded her way through toys and fighting children into Maureen's kitchen. The lunch pots were draining. The sink was full of nappies. A used potty and a box of newly delivered groceries were underfoot. The kitchen clock said three. Christie put the light on. Matthew toddled in. She used part of the kitchen roll to wipe his running nose and then she put the kettle on. She heard Juliette's brisk voice through the partly opened door: 'Oh Dora! A child of three can't comprehend number bonds. She's just repeating parrot fashion.'

'Of course she isn't!'

Christie looked at the clothes waiting to be ironed, the potatoes needing to be peeled, the broken pieces of plastic toy waiting to be swept up. And she was seized by helplessness. Oh God, oh God, oh God. The words repeated, repeated: an invocation to the implacable mighty one. What if life, an alien life, stirred within her?

What if she, too, were trapped in an infinity of lounge-diners?

Rage shook her. Her foot pressed harder on the accelerator.

And then she became aware of something familiar. She knew she was driving by the small row of cottages where she used to live when she was small, before they had moved down into the town to the house on the council estate. Her foot eased back on the pedal.

She imagined her father striding free across the moorland towards Rake Top, towards the mountain. She was stumbling behind him, small but determined, legs tangled up in wet slapping grasses. Every now and then he would remember her presence and turn and wait for her to catch up with him, laughing at her clumsiness, at her wayward, awkward limbs: a laughter brimming with delight, delight that she was his, his daughter. They had never talked much about the mountain. There was no need. He had communicated Rake Top to her silently, with love, and now its mysteries ran through her veins as they had run through his. It was their mountain, their secret, their place of magic.

She could feel the snow under the wheels of her car. She gave a start of surprise as her headlights flickered over the sign 'Owd Bett's'. The inn was high up on the snaking road. She was moving into the backbone of the Pennines.

She went on: on and on, putting more and more distance between her and the women drinking afternoon coffee. Dark Dora's peevishness. 'My God, you'd think he'd get up once to see to our Nicola. Five o'clock on the dot. She always wakes up at that time. And she's been able to climb out of her cot for ages. Of course, I know hyperactive children are intelligent. Everyone says that. But he expects me to be at one of his office do's until the early hours and then see to Nicola a couple of hours later.

I'm worn out. Worn to the bone. But does he care?' The thin voice spilled out of the placid Madonna face, and the spreading of motherly limbs curved in the fatness of the chair. Her sound was like a wasp in clotted cream.

Christie felt the car slide. 'Careful!' She spoke aloud, fear sharpening her voice. The wheels began to bite again. She had seen a road accident once: a man with a face like a pulped orange. She turned up the volume on the radio.

There was such a rawness in the air. Even in the car she could feel it. The wheels began to skid again, so gently, floating. She mustn't put her foot on the brake. Wasn't that right? Faster, faster. Her boot slammed down on the pedal. Her world turned in the windscreen. Her hands flew to shield her face. She pitched forward. There was an explosive brightness in her head. It grew. She felt a dark beyond it: cold, quiet, waiting for her. Am I dying, she wondered; am I going to die? One has to die. Everybody says so.

She reached into the dark, surprised, not yet arrived at fear. The music was still on. The snow slowly changed the nature of the car, making all fantastical.

The cold seeping through the seams of her clothing, seeping through the seams of her until it hurt like a great wound, a martyr's wound. She didn't want to take up the burden of that hurt. She began to cry. Her tears brought awareness of the car, of her predicament, of the fact that she wasn't dead.

'Oh, his car,' she moaned. What would he say about its wrecked presence? How would she placate David? 'What have I done to his car? Oh Christ!'

She tried to move. She gave a shout of pain, leaning back in the dark—hot, frightened, now so full of hurt that she wasn't sure which part of her was injured. Her hands, her arms, seemed all right. Her body, her legs? She groped for her handbag, pulling it towards her. The car trembled. She felt sick. She closed her eyes—so hot, summer-hot. And she and Dora running children. They had tied a rope to the bough of a silver birch and swung out above the valley. Snap of breaking wood, falling, falling.

She came to with a jerk. The car was crashed. David would be very angry. She should never have driven off. That stupid row. All over a telephone bill. She hated rows. She even hated other people's rows. Angry words penetrated her like needles through the skin.

The pain was less. She realised that it came from her left foot. Her ankle? Well, perhaps it was all for the best. If her foot was broken, he couldn't be so angry about the car. Oh God. That silly telephone bill. And now they would have to pay for the Volkswagen to be mended. He'd have to go to work by train. That would put him in a fine temper! 'David. David,' she whispered. Her hand moved hesitantly out, almost as if he were near—there to touch it, there to hold it, there to forgive her. To banish pain. All her pain.

But he wasn't there.

She lay quiet in the limbo of her pain until it came to her that if she stayed where she was she might be frozen to death. Did people die of exposure when in a car? She didn't know. The cold was intense. It hurt almost as much as her ankle. The inn, Owd Bett's, was at least three miles down the road, but there was The Bield, the farmhouse at Rake Bottom. It couldn't be far.

If she shut her eyes, there was home, warm and no pain. She needed magic.

Her father used to make things appear and disappear and seemingly fly through space. 'Anything is possible,' he told his wondering daughter, slyly poking a finger at the elements of life. 'Anything is possible.' 'Except the rent will be paid on a Thursday,' rejoined her mother. Father and daughter smiled at each other. There were scarves to come out of sticks and torn paper to be made whole. But the rent man came too. Christie remembered

9

him clearly. He wore gloves with no fingers in them, and his hands were greasy with the dirt of coins which slid through them into his leather bag.

Perhaps she should wait here, in the car. Perhaps someone would find her. Could she be seen from the road? Oh God, what would she say to David about it all? Justifications collected in a colander at the bottom of her mind. Her fingers formed in a pattern on the steering wheel, like paralysed January twigs.

It seemed so long ago now, the afternoon: a warm, cosy world spinning away from her, and she abandoned in the outer space of this night. The other life: Maureen, sharp-faced, peering at her through myopic China-blue eyes. 'Honestly, Christie. It's nearly boiled dry.' 'What?' 'The kettle.' 'Oh.' Maureen hung against the door of the kitchen like a dangling French bean. 'I mean, it's so terrible. I flood all over the place. All down my back. The ache. It's not right. Not right, to lose clots as big as that. Can't be right. Of course, I've had one D and C. I was in hospital three days. Before Matthew was on the way.' 'I remember you saying. Yes, you told me.' 'And do you think he cares? I tell you, he can't even lay off when I'm unwell. That man would have a poke in a jar of pickles if nothing else was handy.'

Christie found she was crying again. She must get out of the car. She must get help. Gently she eased herself to the door, pushing the lever down. The door dropped away. Snow hit her, and she thrust herself into it, giving a sharp cry as her injured ankle rapped the seat. The snow took her over. She fought it in sudden panic, hitting at its ever-yielding, ever-gaining power. She realised, shame-faced, that it came only to her knees.

Before her was a sharp incline up the road, but she couldn't see where it started or where the roaring sky-line ended. She used the side of the car for support as she began to climb. The pain from her foot was, she discovered, a counterpoint only, an occasional exclamation in her desire to escape. It couldn't be broken, surely.

She lost her grip and slithered into the snow. Its icy wetness filled her nostrils, stopped up her eyes. The sensible thing to do was to wait in the car. Help would come to her. She gritted her teeth and dragged herself up: she wanted to get out of this now.

She reached the road. The slicing snow snapped her half-shut. Bending, groping, shovelling, sliding, she floundered through the night. In her mind's eye was the farmhouse at Rake Bottom, clear and bright, its low stone walls rocked in the endless hazy summer of childhood walks.

The image sustained her as she blundered onwards, and then its last glow trickled out of her mind. So cold, death-cold. David, she thought: the Rugby-playing Englishman who liked his beer, his sport, his car—arrogant, bland, sure of himself and his world. David caressing her neck. He was home. Or at the pub. Drinking pints. Did he already talk of 'the wife'? Or was she still Christie? Was she still Christie to him?

She must think of warm things, hot things, kettle-hot, steaming hot, eiderdown-hot, like her lilac quilt with the purple clematis vulgarly printed on it, wrapping her round and round. She had bought it from the mail-order company when they were first married and living in the attic flat in Bury New Road. Had she and David been different people then? They looked over the roof-tops and fed the birds, and the world seemed so very new, sometimes hurtfully new. She jerked her head into the screaming wind, howling with it.

She went on. She was deadened now and unseeing, but unerringly she felt the road about her. To her left was the tumble-down cowshed at whose summer windows wild white-frilled carrots made a moving curtain, and now she was passing the gap in the dry-stone walls.

The mountain had been her summer playground, and

though she had rarely visited it since her marriage it pervaded what she was, tangible always, like the face of her mother, the rooms of her childhood homes, the teenage vistas of bedraggled paper blowing through monotones of council houses on the estate they had moved to. She might have come into the world naked, she thought, but now she was stitched irrevocably into life. The bent hawthorn was to her right. Beyond was the track to the farm. She moved towards it through the heaving landscape, an iced swimmer.

And then her knowledge was confronted with an alien thing, a tubular iron farmyard gate. She stopped, puzzled by its brisk newness. She tried to open it, but it was locked: she would have to haul herself over it. She felt herself begin to collapse, begin to cry. She straightened her spine. She needed all her will-power, all her concentration, to hoist her body above its bars and down the other side.

The gate led directly into the farmyard. An oak, whose airborne roots stood out like a skirt, survived by the door of the house. Its moaning was monotonous, an endless soughing of ancient, hurting branches. There was a new brass knocker on the door and she used it. No answer. She tried the latch, and the door opened easily. She let herself in.

'Is anyone there!' she shouted into the darkness.

A gust of wind pulled the door out of her grasp, and it crashed to. The darkness was warm, she discovered.

'Is anyone there!'

Her voice was hardly carried. She tried to shout again, but the words formed in her head were too tired to reach her lips. All broken up, she thought, as she slid towards the floor. He'll be so angry.

Warm, warm. Radiators—that's it, there must be radiators, central heating. Oh dear, no one here.

She began to dream. She was sinking to the bottom of a tropical sea. She was aware of anxieties, of dangers, but they were receding and the shark with the Volkswagen grin seemed almost amiable. Now she was on a train, going through flat countryside, Ormskirk countryside, where the potatoes grew. She was travelling home from university at the end of term. The sky was sullen overhead and bolts of wind flattened wedges of potato crop. And then a tunnel and the noise of the train growing louder and louder, drum-di-drum, drum-di-drum, in her ears.

She awoke, becoming aware of the furious throbbing in her ankle. She sat up and leant protectively over the injury.

'Is anyone here!' she shouted. 'Hey!'

There was no answer.

What had been a solid dark was now many shapes, a brass-faced grandfather clock, a radiator, boots, walking sticks in a rack.

'Hello!'

No answer.

Well, at least it was quite warm. But why was it warm? Where were the people living in this house? She lifted her head, listening carefully. The clock, a noise in the pipes, the shifting bones of the house, a closed, intimate quietness, its outer rim shuddering with the sounds of blizzard. No human sound. She must find something to deaden the pain in her ankle. Aspirins. It was going to be difficult to move, so she must think carefully. Medicine chest? In the bathroom, probably, and that meant upstairs. She looked doubtfully at her boot. Was it a break or a sprain? If she bound it tight with a wet bandage perhaps it wouldn't hurt so much. And these clothes. She must get into something dry. She found she was weeping. Why was no one here, no one to help her?

Carefully she manoeuvred herself to the bottom of the stairs and felt them. Polished wood, open tread. Newly installed? Using her sound leg as a lever she pushed herself off the floor into a sitting position on the bottom stair. Now that she had come out of the snow, now she had escaped, her leg, her pain, dominated her conscious thrust. But she hadn't been worried by it—had she?—snow-blind by the tubular iron gate? Fretfully she pushed hair out of her face.

Even as she worked herself up the stairs, her purpose was burrowed into by other anxieties. There was something strange about this house. Like, like ... What was it that wasn't right? Leaving the central heating on while they were out? David wouldn't like that. She thought of him with his anorak over his business suit, and gritted her teeth. Groceries, hoovering, bills, gas, rates. A gnawing at the vitals, a knowledge that she hadn't bothered to pay for the papers for three months. Oh, the time when he was undiscovered territory, when Eden lay hidden beyond the upward curve of flesh!

Soft carpet on the landing: wool in her fingers. She dug her nails into the pile and was reminded of the feel of David's school blazer, his shape before he got solid shoulders. He used to be so thin, his Adam's apple stuck out, making him bird-like, turkey-like. She saw him under the misty lamp-post eating a bar of chocolate he had bought from his grandma's sweet shop. He often came after school. 'Got a beau, eh? A young man?' Grandma grinned, her face the texture of old newspaper but her eyes undimmed, triumphant prisms of reflecting light. 'Your first beau. What does your mother say to that?' 'I don't like him!' she yelled, perhaps sensing, even then, the cell door slamming. 'Anyway, he's got spots.' 'You take *my* advice. Don't be fussy where men are concerned. Take your mother. She picked and fussed until she got a man as fine-looking as any you'll see—and a fat lot o' good it did 'er.'

'She drove him away,' Christie said between clenched teeth.

'That's as may be.'

'She tried to kill the magic in him.'

14

'Silly tricks. That's what it were. Good-f'-nothing tricks. A man needs a job at his back when he's bringing up a family. Your grandfer now, 'ee were a carpenter. Things 'ee could make! Pride, in them days. Pride and skill goes together. He carved dolls f' your mother and Auntie Freda, two beautiful dolls. 'Ee were such a patient man and to see them things come alive in yon hands … Now that were magic, proper magic. Rabbits from 'ats! That's deceiving, that is. Doesn't last, tricks. Nothing f' yer effort. Nowt solid t' see. I've still got them dolls. Your mam wanted me to let you 'ave 'em but I wouldn't.'

'Why not?'

'Them dolls are 'im, to me they are. What's left o' yon man.' She rubbed her fingers along her flank. 'When I see t' dolls I sees freckles on his 'ands too.'

'You loved him?' Christie was startled.

'Aye'

'But I loved *my* father. I carry the things he did in my head. I carry him in my head!'

But did she? Christie frowned. Would she now recognise her father if she passed him on the street?

Sometimes she looked at men, thinking 'Is that him?' and panic would fill her and blot out all her images of him. He was gone. She still remembered the clothes he had left, neatly bundled up and ready for the Salvation Army. People did that when someone died, but of course he wasn't dead. Just gone. Walked out on them.

She could make out the square linoleum tiles of the bathroom. She would have to reach up for the light. She sniffed the warm air. There was something … something about this house. Deep in her, buried beneath reason, almost beyond consciousness was a primitive … she couldn't say. She tried to sniff it out, tried to catch its elusive scent. There was something … but no, she couldn't clothe her apprehension.

She snapped the light on. The sanitary ware was avocado-green and gleamed expensively. She found

15

aspirin in the medicine chest and took four. Gingerly she removed her boot. The ankle was swollen, but not as much as she had imagined. She bound it tightly with a crepe bandage, and the initial spurts of pain were reduced to a dull throb. She leaned against the bath, worried about changing out of her wet clothes. What would the owner think when he came back to find her not only in his house, but in his clothes too? She shrugged helplessly. It couldn't be helped. She stripped away the chilly dampness of sheepskin, sweater and slacks and left them heaped in the bathroom.

The bedroom was incredibly ship-shape—books, objects, clothes arranged so meticulously that she was sure the room's occupant would know if anything were touched.

The linen lay in a mahogany chest of drawers, which smelled of cool summer breezes, of full blown, billowing grasses. She selected an old, but scrupulously clean, pair of jeans from the bottom drawer and a sweater. The man was small, she discovered, but, thank God, had a reasonably-sized posterior. He was quite plump, judging from the folds of denim at her waist. She hoisted the jeans to with a belt and added another sweater to the first.

She sat on the bed. Her exertions had left her shaky and unsure. This house ... did it exist at all? The room was so hot and cloudy, meticulous objects moving with a sudden life of their own. The bands of colour became brighter and she felt herself falling back on the bed. The heat of summer and the voluptuous curve of dock—it thrust its sappy stem high, its root deep, evil in its greedy intent ... dead white winter hands and slush-smashed snow. And through the glittering fragments a single image emerged. She was stunned by its simplicity. A telephone! Of course. She could ring David. A house which had open-tread stairs and a wool carpet—this house was bound to have a telephone.

Rain swilling relentlessly down and underwear

16

steaming dry on the old maiden by the fire, biscuit mottled tiles and brown teapot on the chrome-plated stand—no telephone *there*: no telephone in her mother's house. Where was the telephone in this house? In the hall? She began to cry. How would she get back down those stairs? She was so very tired, aching tired. She lay helpless, aware she must move, but not moving.

Her tears slowly dried on her cheeks. All those regimented lines of masculine belongings. Six cuff links, she counted. Gold? Three fishing rods, a holy trinity. She stirred restlessly.

It could have been worse. She wasn't dead. There were aeons of deadness, but she hadn't died when she crashed the car. And yet she felt an unbearable sadness. She sighed as she eased herself off the bed. When she was young life had stretched about her like a sky, full of freedom and emptiness, and she could rise up in it like a lark. Wordsworth knew all about that, and all about afterwards too—when that sky was a pin-head and less. Perhaps youth is the only immortality. Perhaps immortality was something you grew out of when you had a house with a lounge-diner. Angrily she pushed herself through the bedroom door and went downstairs.

She groped for the hall light and snapped it on. The brass face of the grandfather clock showed ten minutes to ten. So many hours gone. Where was the owner of this house? She needed looking after.

'Is anyone there!' A man. A man's house. She had known that from the first, she realised. Why was she so sure? 'Is anyone there!' she shouted again.

She hardly waited. She knew there would be no answer. Manouevring over to the telephone, she picked up the receiver and dialled her home number, muttering with impatience. It was some time before she realised there was no ringing sound. She jammed the receiver down, picked it up again and listened. No sound. Oh God. The blizzard must have brought the lines down. She tried again. It was no use.

Why was no one in this house? She felt a growing anger. 'Hey there!' she yelled. 'Where are you?'

What noise was that? She listened intently. 'The wind in the tree by the door,' she sighed. She took a walking stick and found herself far more mobile.

'Is anyone there!'

She listened again. Her concentration was so great that she could hear her own body working, and now she pushed her perception out into distant corners, closed cupboards. She discerned nothing, gave up and decided to investigate the ground floor.

First, she found the lounge, a big, low-slung room. A log fire still burned brightly in the stone hearth. The depths of its glow changed almost imperceptibly from moment to moment, world merging into new world, and then crash, and sparks splintered into outer darkness and the process began all over again. The sulphur smell permeated faintly upwards to the heavily beamed ceiling. The parquet floor was slippery underfoot and shadowed with the reflecting shapes of furniture.

On a glass-topped table was a montage of bird skeletons, caught in amber perspex. Slowly but steadily she moved closer to it. Juxtaposed against the skeletons was a picture of a middle-aged woman, the shadow of a bird's claw falling across her face. She turned to study the books and listened again. What was it? Who was it? Was the wind cracking the spine of the house? She shivered slightly. A neat row of pebbles winked at her obsessively from the oak of a wide mantelshelf. She succumbed to an impulse to scatter the stones' order and looked with satisfaction at the disarray she caused. 'He's a nut,' she decided. 'His finger-nails will be beautifully looked after. Dorian Grey.'

She tried to shake the images off. She thought of her own home—the brown and orange G-Plan lounge and her agitation at discovering its twin on the estate where she lived. Mass taste and the feeling of loss ... loss of what? Identity? She now disliked the room she had chosen with such care.

She looked down at the stones again, almost sorry that she had disturbed them.

Again she circled the coffee table. The bird montage didn't seem so hostile a thing now. But wasn't there something paranoid about all these close collections of objects?

Abruptly she left the lounge, moving briskly with the aid of the stick. She opened a door at the bottom of the hall and put the light on. She saw chairs, Windsor wheel-back, and the gingham check of a table cloth, and what looked like the remains of a meal.

She moved closer. The table had been set for two. But it wasn't the *remains* of a meal she saw but one that hadn't even been started. There was steak, two vegetables. French fried onions in a small tureen, a bottle of vin rosé. A chair lay on its side on the floor. Nothing else was disturbed. Two candles, guttering, were still alight.

Christie was aware of a tightening in her limbs, a physical shrivelling. She stood very still, slowly surveying the table again, and each dish of that uneaten meal sank through layer and layer of consciousness.

2

Burning caverns. The smell of fire, smoke on her tongue, heat on her cheeks and her mother almost asleep, a work-worn hand chipping at the varnish on the chair arm. It was all so safe, with the rain and the gloom shut out by panes which reflected their content. The moving shadows on old wallpaper and her mother's hand touching, caressing her head, making a miracle, a shivering, shimmering rainbow encompassing their world and then gone. The dog's nose half under her bottom and her feet stinging with pins and needles when she moved.

There it was again. Barking. But Mick was dead. He went out one night when he was old and fat and never came back. Her mother said he'd gone out to die. That's what they did, she said. Dogs never died indoors if they could help it.

Christie jerked up, now fully awake. She was on the sofa in the lounge, which she had positioned so that she could get a better view of the door. She hadn't meant to go to sleep.

Earlier she had shut the door on the dining room, closing off the sight of the uneaten meal. Again she picked up the telephone. She must get through to David. She needed to hear his voice. But the line was dead, quite dead. She dialled and dialled into nothing.

And then her eye lit on the cream snake of wire on the brick-hued tiles of the hall floor. The line had been severed. Neat—no mess, no ripping away. A planned violence, a violence so decorous she noticed it only then.

Bending down to examine the total disconnection, she took each wire in her hands and experimentally joined them together again. The thread of their severance couldn't be healed, but remained. She was overwhelmed by a feeling of helplessness. She stayed on her knees, the wires in her hand, and waited—waited to be sucked up in the chaos which was crushing the walls of The Bield. Would the roof crash, the windows stove in? How would darkness descend on her?

Then, with the help of the walking stick, she determinedly got to her feet. She could have no understanding of the uneaten meal, the sliced telephone wire. But she would face whatever this night brought her, or didn't bring.

She went into the lounge and repaired the fire, patiently coaxing the flames. But when her hand touched a burning log she didn't feel it. Later, when a small blister arose, she was to wonder how it got there.

The wind shook the windows. The glass squealed in its frames. The dog barked again, a dog somewhere outside in unholy night. Did it belong to the house? Its howling was frantic. Was it slowly being entombed in snow —like the vegetables entombed in their tureens in the dining room? The broccoli had been pretty. It lay in gentle greenness in the cream dish, not quite cold. She shivered. The dog outside was whining now. Would her husband cry at her funeral as she had at her grandma's? 'Funeral?' she mocked herself. 'Stop being bloody ridiculous!' She remembered the black limousine swinging round the curve in the municipal cemetery and how the blue neon cross on the concrete spire buried itself in her stomach. She hadn't cried when she first knew of her grandma's death, but she cried then. It was so unfair, the impact that symbol of Christ had on an unbeliever, and afterwards it was always a symbol of her impermanence, of a suddenly happened upon consciousness which would be annihilated just as abruptly. She could have died a few hours earlier in her crashed car. She might die before this night was over. That was what she was waiting for, wasn't it? That was why her spine sought protection from the back of the sofa. Her thought snapped. She was only aware of the glistening lumps of her hand on the walking stick.

The wind had battered the chapel the day her grandma's body was cremated. There was the awful moment when the conveyor belt gave a little jerk, and then came into motion again, and her grandma's coffin was despatched into the flame. It was a moment of such inevitability, such dignity, that it shook the congregation. And it was a mystery at such odds with the cross-grained old woman who made a habit of losing her Last Will and Testament and who kept pennies warming on the mantelshelf—'for my eyes'—she told her granddaughter with relish.

'You won't be dead for a long time yet!' Christie shouted. Her grandma thrust her hands on bony hips, as she always did when angry. Her eyes were monkey-bright. 'I'll be gone. Come next spring. Next summer. In the time it takes to blink.'

'Oh, shut up! We won't get rid of you so easily.' Christie bit deep and hard into the apple the old woman had given her.

And grandma, suddenly despairing, sank into the armchair. Tough, sinewy fingers, which had carried out such purposeful work, wandered aimlessly on her skirt. 'Old bones, old fears, old shadows ... it will come soon. Soon now! I can smell it.' Gripping at the chair she added: 'What do the young know? What do the young know about it, eh? You think you will live forever, but it will catch up on you. There. Waiting. You run and run and run through the years but it is there. Waiting. And it's all over. All in the blink of an eye.'

'Well, that blink's already lasted seventy-two years.'

Christie demolished the remaining apple. The core was already browning.

'Ha. Huh! The young always think the world belongs to them. A seventy-two-year-old ought to climb into the coffin and give 'em more space! Nature's using you, my girl, to give her more children who'll thrust you down the dark 'ole.'

'Grandma, I love you. We all do.'

But her grandma wouldn't be consoled. Next day she had gone to the cemetery to preview the coming events. She told Christie she felt cheated, enraged, that she couldn't be present at her own funeral. Here was this ritual, this drama, in which she was the heroine and she wouldn't be there to savour it. It put her in a fury.

A bus conductor made her even more furious when he put her off at the wrong stop and she had an extra half-mile walk. Dying was forgotten for a week or two. But of course it did come quite soon. Grandma's sense of smell hadn't let her down.

What did she mean? Smell it? Can I smell it? Christie wondered. Do I perceive it here, in this place, in The Bield? Oh, that damned dog. Why doesn't it stop howling!

Is my death coming? Soon? Can I really smell it? When she heard the dog barking again it was a friendly sound. Anything was better than the vast, incomprehensible reaches of emptiness which destroyed her boundaries. She felt herself becoming disembodied, indistinguishable from her surroundings.

She tried to hold on to herself, to pluck herself back from the invading room. There was a perfectly reasonable explanation for the uneaten meal. A sudden crisis ... the people called away. Why, they even left the central-heating on and logs burning in the grate. But the cut telephone wire?

She tried a different logic. There was no one here. The house was empty. How can you be harmed if there is no stairway. She picked it up: a lipstick with the top off—a pale, unattractive shade in the harsh light of day.

There was no sign of the top. Someone applying it in the bathroom? ... running downstairs. But why? Her heart lurched. It's all conjecture, she thought. She reached the bottom of the stairs, and avoided looking at the telephone.

Yes. She must get out of this place. She jammed the lipstick in her pocket. There was a sound above her and she straightened her shoulders, swinging round to confront what she might find. She could see nothing.

'Who's there?'

The dog appeared, stretched itself and yawned. It stretched itself again and scratched its side. Time monotonously unwound, reeling off the ticking face of the grandfather clock.

She sank on the stairs. 'What's the matter with me?' she asked the dog. 'What's wrong? What else could it be but you? What's the matter with me? The night is over now.'

Light, pooled in the centre of the hall, was running to its outer edges, defining the blur of shadows, revealing hidden corners with prosaic reality.

She opened the front door and gasped. The snow was waist-high—glittering, stodgy, sickening, like mountains of icing sugar. She stuck an exploring finger in it. 'It must have drifted against the walls.' The cold was beginning to settle in her hands and feet. Small, extreme bones moaned and stirred. She felt dizzy. 'I'm hungry,' she discovered, surprised. 'Look, dog. Look at the snow.'

The dog looked and didn't like it. It whimpered.

'That's exactly how I feel,' she said. She shut the door, stamping her feet and letting her hands curl under her jersey. 'Let's find the kitchen.' Daylight and the thought of food made her feel quite cheerful, and she decided to give the dog the rest of the uneaten meal. 'Once you've had that, I'll feel happier,' she told it. 'I'll know it's been

35

one to harm you? Images couldn't harm you. There were no people here. This house was empty. The hairs at the nape of her neck stirred. Someone could come. That was why she was waiting, wasn't it? That was why she held on to the walking stick so tightly.

But why should anyone want to harm her? She hadn't seen anything, hadn't witnessed any event. What had there been to witness? 'Jesus Christ,' she whispered. 'What's happened?'

She found she was longing to see, to touch, the barking dog. She needed something live, outside herself. Why didn't she get that dog and bring it in? Perhaps it would let her hug it, let her bury her head in its fur.

She had tried to get out before, to escape from The Bield. She had pulled the front door open, but stings of howling snow had blinded her. Blasts of wind driving her back.

No one was going to do anything to her, she thought in relief. Who could get through a night like this? If she was cut off from the outside world, the outside world was cut off from her. What had put the thought of death in her head? Perhaps it was some kind of bizarre psychological response to finding herself alive after the car crash.

Still, there was nothing wrong in getting that dog. It was the humane thing. It could get buried in the snow. She remembered her terrier, Mick. He had a way of thrusting his nose up through her fingers when he wanted to lay his head on her lap. Her eye caught the careful arrangements of bird skeletons. Would a man as meticulous as this own a dog? And she'd seen no trace of a dog basket; there was no smell of dog about this house. It wasn't the owner's dog—suddenly she felt sure of that.

'Perhaps it was a woman who arranged the bird skeletons,' she murmured to herself, but she couldn't think so. Women didn't like dead things: man was the destroyer. She thought of her mother. She thought of the shell which was left when her father ran out on them, abandoning them in the depths of that council estate. He left a woman behind him whose life was suddenly without purpose, a life which became incapable of generating warmth, only of stealing it, stealing the warmth of others.

She remembered how it was when she was very small and they were living in the stone cottage which backed onto the moor. She had been in bed recovering from some childish ailment, peevish, demanding. Her mother had sat at the edge of the bed, knitting clothes for her doll, her presence soothing ointment, fingers sometimes touching, tending, caring. Patiently she was fed milk jellies and rice puddings and told her favourite fairy tales in a slow, halting voice—for her mother wasn't an educated woman and though she could read perfectly well she couldn't find the confidence in her to speak the written word without hesitation. It was as if she felt she had no right to the knowledge that lay in the pages of books.

She found herself listening for the dog, that live, demanding noise. She became more and more distressed when she couldn't hear it. 'I must get it.' The pain in her foot made her wince as she hurried to the door. The grandfather clock struck two.

By the front door she hesitated. Perhaps the dog had gone away. If it really didn't belong to the house, whose was it? Was the owner near? She oughtn't to open the door. She didn't know what she might be letting in. Her fingers trembled as she turned the handle. The wind slapped the door back against the wall. Howling blackness engulfed her. 'Here, here! Here, dog, here!' Her voice was snatched away from her, tossed up in a swirl of snow. Was the creature already dead? Could anything survive in such a night? 'Here! Come on in. Here, here!' If she left the door jammed open and went away, it might sneak in. And all the demons of the night with it.

The wet bundle hurtled past her, and she slammed the door shut.

She looked at the dog. It looked at her. It was friendly. It began to shake the wet out of its coat and it went on shaking, showering the hall so that ice mist glittered and danced and was absorbed into warm, dark shadow. 'Whose are you? To whom do you belong?' It had a collar, but no tag. Abstractedly she ran a troubled hand through her hair. She was so tired. Perhaps she could sleep now that the dog was here. That was what she needed: sleep, to be absorbed into quiet. The dog would watch over her. It would bark if anyone came. Of course the dog didn't belong to the house. Now that it had stopped shaking out the night it sniffed around. She bent to make sure that there was no tag attached to its collar. 'I suppose you're hungry. You want your supper.' She felt an urge to care for it, to show it how grateful she was that it was there. 'Come on, then.' She was so tired, she was dizzy with tiredness. Perhaps the meal didn't exist after all, perhaps all of this was just an invention of her fatigue.

She opened the dining-room door. The meal lay with sepulchral quietness on the table, but it didn't frighten her any more. 'At least I'm not going out of my mind,' she told the dog. 'It's all here. The untouched food.' The gingham tablecloth was green and toned in with the vegetables. Had the cook been aware of that when he chose it?

She went round the table and righted the wheel-backed chair which had crashed to the floor. Things looked less unusual already.

'Would you like some supper?' The dog cocked his ears. 'Well, I'm afraid it's cold.'

Selecting steak and some vegetables, she arranged them on a plate, which she put on the floor. The dog gazed up at her and then gingerly snuffled round the plate. 'Go on. You can. Unless it's poisoned.' She was laughing at herself, her fears. The plate danced across the striped rug. She felt pleased. 'You're eating up a nightmare. Did you know that? Gobble, gobble. All gone. I'll drink it up. God, I wish I had a cigarette. I wish I'd remembered to bring my cigarettes with me.' She picked up the bottle of rosé and took a swig. She was beginning to get excited. David and she had once lain together on a grave. He'd wanted to make love to her, but she hadn't let him, frightened of releasing the Devil. 'But now we're eating him up,' she laughed. 'That's what we're doing! Eating the Devil up. Drinking him up too!' And then she was apprehensive, for what fate was she tempting?

She listened, trying to catch the shadows of night. She moved to the wall, protecting her back. The walking stick was held to bar the way to her stomach. 'Oh God, I'm being ridiculous again. I'm just so tired I can't think straight!'

The plate banged into the table leg, and the dog gave a yelp as he skittered into it. There was a lull in the storm and she became aware of the noise the animal's teeth made as it champed on flesh. Such a charming little thing, too. All brown and white fur and trusting golden eyes.

The dog was becoming less frantic now. It must have finished the meat. She noticed a large brown spot on the gingham cloth near the crashed chair. Was it wine? Yes, of course it was. She moved away from the wall and carefully walked round the table. She lifted the wine bottle and deliberately dribbled a bit on the cloth, waiting for the stain to dry. She was patient, with an ancestral patience, like a woman moving through a death watch.

The dog nosed out from under the table and rubbed an appreciative head against her leg and then licked its chops. The dried wine stain wasn't the same as the other.

'I think I'll go to sleep,' she told the dog. 'I'm really very tired. Come with me.' All the same she was surprised

27

when the dog came, and grateful. 'Is your owner outside?' she whispered. But the house was quiet, a little box of stillness spinning through the spaces of her dread.

The clocks struck three, one after the other, and she was careful as she climbed the stairs. She thought of the people in the afternoon—Maureen, Juliette, Dora, in their conjugal beds, safe. She thought of Dora as she had known her as a schoolgirl, a mop of woolly hair thrusting up from her head like a black halo. They had been studying Michelangelo's *David*.

'It's so small. It's no bigger than my finger. You can see that.'

'Ah,' Dora said. 'It grows.'

'What makes it grow?'

'It just shoots up.'

'What makes it shoot up?'

Dora, cross: 'How do I know! It fills up with air. Like a balloon.' Her coffee eyes were slits of light.

'How big does it get?'

'Like a salami.'

Christie had quietly contemplated this, distantly aware of the uncorking of bottles in a disused cellar of her being. 'What makes it fill with air?'

'When a man gets excited things open up and it gets down there.'

'Goodie!' she thought, not tasting the nectar but feeling out for it, a guest at a future party. 'I wonder what it's like, what it feels like.'

'Are we going to play tennis tonight?'

'I suppose so.'

Dora didn't hear her answer. 'You know? You know what I would really like? I'd like to see the Amazon and the snows of the Arctic. I'd like to know the world as I know our avenue.'

Dust and chalk stirred in the room as a distant door slammed. The sun slanted through a geranium on the window-sill so that the petals shook in a glistening delight. Christie sighed contentedly and began to watch the ladybird move across her thumbnail. She was tranquil in a delight of her own, absorbing everything, lazy in simmering summer.

'Are we going to play tennis tonight?' Dora asked.

'Yes.'

'It's going to be different for me.' Dora was determined. 'I'd like to see India, too.'

'You'll marry, have kids and live in this town. Like us all.' Christie poked the David. The ladybird momentarily stopped in its endless travels and then continued. 'Our future is limited to him.' But that had been a limitless thought, hadn't it? As strange as any Amazon, any India, as wondering as Arctic ice-flows. All lost, somehow, gone—in early morning toast, gas bills and cleaning the lavatory. All quite gone.

'Dog, are you married?'

The dog wagged its tail.

She shrugged her weary shoulders. 'Oh well, it's not so bad really. It's getting used to it that's bad.'

She thought of the long march of childhood, of holidays at her aunt's and the indescribable pleasure of smelling alyssum which grew in a dry bank by the kitchen garden. Knocked you over, that's what it did.

It wasn't a wine stain. What was it? What had stained the gingham tablecloth?

'Who do you belong to?' she suddenly shouted at the dog.

It backed off.

'What's your name? You haven't even got a name!' She stared at it in frustration. 'Oh. I'm going to sleep,' she muttered. The crudely tied up jeans were coming down. She'd wake up with David at her side and perhaps she would count his backbones or continue to worry about the small bald patch on his head which was taking an increasingly large hold on her imagination.

She chose a bedroom at random. She didn't switch on

the light because the fastidious arrangements of furniture and objects bore heavily on her, overlaying her, like thickening frost on leaf.

As she gave herself up to the bed and was nearly asleep, she remembered the fragrance of alyssum. It wasn't something out of her past, something that grew in Aunt Freda's garden, she realised. It was there—now—rising above the stairs. What? Aftershave or perfume? Some draught had wafted the scent into her nostrils. From where? What?

No one was in the house. She was sure—almost sure. Of course no one was in the house. Her arms moved quietly, protectively, across her body. The shadows in the room grew colder by the minute: the central heating must have shut down for the night. She became more aware of the pain from her ankle. Her body, too, had its own ache, a dull, tired, frustrated ache. Where did the fragrance come from? She surveyed the darkness from the bed. The dog's disembodied eyes met hers and then floated through the air and disappeared. She heard the animal settle under the bed. His shuffling limbs warmed her. 'I like dogs,' she realised. 'I missed our dog when he died. I missed Mick. Of course he was greedy. He sat in the middle of people's lawns and begged when he could see them round their dinner tables. But he always barked when he heard strangers. Nice and loud. He ate the postman's leg.' She heard the dog whine and smiled to herself.

Her aunt grew gladioli as well as alyssum. She had a lodger who had taken part in the Battle of Arnhem. Sometimes he screamed in the night, sometimes he appeared in the morning with a face like a ripped-up flower. Aunt Freda said he drank the whisky in the bottles piled up in the dustbin, but her pudgy, flushed cheeks and glittering eye made a liar of her.

'Our Freda's troubles are all 70 per cent proof,' Christie's mother observed cynically. But Aunt Freda lived by the sea and didn't mind them spending a week or two with her in the summer, so Christie's mother overlooked her sister's vice. 'A child needs a bucket and spade once a year, so I put up with our Freda. I put up with everything. You've got to, when there's no choice. The rights and wrongs o' things aren't for likes o' us. They're for people who can afford them. Grand ideas need grand bank balances.' When Christie was a teenager she thought her mother was born to be poor and deserted, for no other way of living suited her nature so much. If it was sunny it was too dry, if rainy, too wet, a gift was always the wrong colour, or size or shape, and if she won any money on a horse it would be too little for what she wanted to buy. 'Your ma,' Grandma said, not mincing matters, 'is like the potato blight that did for yon Irish buggers.' It wasn't that her mother was a killjoy, Christie thought, rather that she took her joys perversely, revelling in the sourness of life.

And yet her mother hadn't always been like that, Christie realised. In the dank kitchen of their moorland cottage her hands had danced in the big pot mixing bowl, flour singing through the air as she made short crust pastry for schools of crimped maids-of-honour which would decorate the table at tea time. When the man in their life went away, though, the gleaming light which darted through her mother's movements had slowly, almost imperceptibly, faded away. She was like a fruit tree with no water to suck into its roots, to bring forth the blossoms, the fruit.

Grandma, though, liked neither this daughter nor her other daughter, Freda. What affection was left in her went out to Christie, and Christie found her past in the old woman and her tales of what life was like before she was born.

Christie thought of the skin that was too large for the worn bones of the old woman's hands, remembered how it puckered like badly sewn material and how beautiful she had thought those hands. There were times when her grandmother dazzled in a beauty and the girl never sorted out the dreadful contradictions of the ugliness and smell of old age, the decaying of life, and her occasional visions of over-powering splendour and rightness.

At last she slept, lulled by the domestic images of her past into a healing quiet.

What woke her she didn't know, but the dark wasn't total any more and the storm which had rattled the teeth of the old house had given up its savage hold. Time whirred with a refrigerator purr. Her limbs shuffled closer together for warmth. There was a misty jumble of shapes which were slowly individualising, slowly creating themselves into objects. Beyond was a glow which must be the window. There was an expectancy in the air, the sharp feeling of coming light. So cold. The heating hadn't come on yet. As her mind shrugged off sleep, she stirred restlessly. The dog under the bed sighed. David must have called the police by now. She couldn't feel him. She couldn't reach out to him.

Where was she? Whose house was this? There must be letters and things. She could discover a person, if only secondhand. Perhaps fear would finally leave her if she could somehow know the owner of The Bield. How had he got the bird skeletons for the montage? Did he wait to find the corpses, or had he shot live birds down? The feathers and flesh. Was it boiled off, or did maggots pick the bones clean? The manner of the man ... killing birds was so impossible for her to imagine. It was easier to comprehend the murder of a person. Then passion came into it.

Perhaps it had stopped snowing. Perhaps she could get out of this place. David would be so angry about his car. But it would be all right. She would make it right between them.

Yes, she must get out of this place. Could she do it? She felt a growing excitment, a feeling of impending release.

She thrust both her feet on the bedroom floor and gave a cry of pain. Ineffectual tears ran down her cheeks. Pushing them away, she bent to feel her ankle gingerly. The dog's head loomed beyond the bedspread and gazed up inquiringly.

'It hurts,' she snapped. 'It must be seized up. Oh, I could do with a fag.'

The dog yawned.

She felt like kicking it. Perhaps the thought reached it. It withdrew its head. She reached out for the walking stick. Carefully she eased herself up. The jeans she had slept in sagged about her hips. She hoisted them up again, securing the denim under the belt, and hobbled over to the window. The air was crystal, with such a pure coldness that she gasped. The window was like a pool. Thick snow and frost curved about the outer rim, thinning to the centre, when it suddenly became clear. She peered through this giant eye, looking upwards, out into the world.

It was so still: it was so still it was eerie. Like a dream, she thought. The oak raised howling arms to the sky, unmoving, petrified in its agony. She found it fantastical: like something inward, something at the centre of being. Nothing stirred: no bird, no twig, no life.

But imperceptibly it was growing lighter, and soon the whole scene began to move, light spinning through the coming morning like rays through opal. She felt dazed. She retreated—so lonely, with such a sensation of losing the world. She became immobilised, as still as all the still things in the room, and only the light grew and moved: morning wouldn't be denied.

So lonely. Blighted by loneliness. You always had hope when you were a child, something to reach out to. Everything would be all right when you grew up. The future held your answer. And when an infinity of aspirations became finite and all dreams were fled, what then? Had that happened to her mother?

It was light in the room now, a grey, dull uniform light weighing all the objects with its heavy clarity. She moved slightly back from the window, trying to recapture past magic. Brilliant light suddenly flashed in her eyes. She blinked. It was gone.

Leaning forward, she peered anxiously through the centre of the pool. Was it an electric torch? From the barn? Someone was in the barn. But of course someone was. All dogs had owners. Relief flooded through her. It was another human being, someone there—near—someone in the same predicament as herself, someone to help her. Together they would manage it, manage to dig out from the house and get down to the road.

She peered through the window again. All was still. All was fantastical. Had she imagined that beam of light? Was it, after all, a sudden burst of sun on the window of the barn? Tears of disappointment sprang to her eyes. Now she was frantically looking for signs of life. But it was still—as though the world had stopped. There was no one there after all, no one near.

Oh God. Now she was weeping because she really was alone, alone at The Bield. Last night she had been terrified because she thought someone else could be there, hovering in the chaos: some presence, some bringer of darkness. What a fool she'd been!

But there was the uneaten meal, the cut telephone wire. She shrugged them off. She wouldn't think of them. It was daylight now. There were things to do.

She must make some effort to get out of this place, escape. Suddenly she felt free and full of plans. Could she really reach the road, though? The thought hovered on the fringe to her rapid appraisal of possibilities. There would be a way though. She'd get back down to the town.

She climbed down the stairs and stopped. The smell of ... like alyssum when the rain had stopped, wild delight. A small light object had rolled to the side of the teak

there, but it isn't as bad as having to keep looking at it—if you see what I mean.'

David would be really worried now and he would worry her mother, a common feeling for once stitching the two together. Christie was uneasy, not wanting to think of their misery, their unspoken fears.

'They don't normally even bother to hide their dislike of each other,' she told the dog. David spent most of his time in her mother's presence behind the *Guardian* while her mother erected a *Sun* barrier. If their eyes did involuntarily meet, the shock of their mutual dislike confused them both and warmth drained out of the room like water from a bath tub. 'I suppose he'll make a good husband. Well, anyway, he's got a steady job,' she told her daughter, not saying, never saying, how much she held him in contempt. 'I'll not clear out the spare room, though.'

'I love him, mother!' Christie had been a bride at the time.

'You shouldn't have got married. Young slip of a thing like you. What do you want to go and do a thing like that for? I'd have thought you had more sense. What with Women's Lib and everything. We didn't have that in my day. Or the Pill.'

Christie was shocked. 'You'd rather I'd had an affair?'

'With 'im!' Her mother was scornful. But she didn't meet her daughter's eye. 'Too young. Too young to marry. That's all I say. All that university education gone to waste.' And she added stubbornly. 'No need to marry these days.'

'I love David.' And yet Christie caught her mother's unspoken thought. David wasn't like her father. David had no magic in him. And she saw in her mind's eye all the kites her father used to fashion for her, made out of balsa wood and green tissue paper and how they cavorted through the bowling sky.

'She was right,' she reluctantly told the dog. 'I think

I've married a mediocre man. My father was never that. He had a—a largeness of spirit.'

They were in the dining room now, and she slapped the remaining cold steak in front of the dog. Saliva slid and gleamed on soft, furry jowls. The dog's stare was transfixed by the meat.

She went on into the kitchen. It was a long, galley-like room with black-and-white checked floor carefully matching checked curtains. Just by the door logs for the fire were stacked. Two were tipped on the tiles near the sink unit, as though they had fallen from holding arms. She wasn't in the mood for any more mysteries. Night had gone. It was day. She picked up the logs and placed them on the pile by the door. But she couldn't help noticing, too, the rack of knives fastened to the wall: light bounced viciously off the cutting edges. One of the medium-sized carvers was missing. Well, it would be in the kitchen somewhere, she thought. Probably in the washing-up bowl.

Determinedly she wrapped a butcher's apron about her. With a business like air she looked out of the window to gauge the depth of snow at this side of the house. It was, if anything, deeper. Turning her back on the rack of knives, she opened the refrigerator and took out bacon and eggs. In an earthenware crock she found a loaf.

On a serving tray there was a compote of fruit, with biscuits and cheese. The last course of the uneaten meal? That dog would eat the fruit, too, she thought grimly.

The cooking of eggs and bacon set up a wonderful spitting smell, and she forced a hum out of herself. Selecting a fish slice from the knife rack, she slid her breakfast on to a plate.

There were so many simple pleasures in life, she thought, as she let the yolk run over the bacon. One evening last summer, she remembered, the sun had gone to melted butter. She and David were walking, and all was liquid gold between them. She had been surprised to discover that even just the two of them strolling along could be such a physical unity.

She sighed and leaned back, replete. The grey in the window at the shadowy back of the house was now infusing blue, the dull clarity of the kitchen beginning to glint and frizzle at the edges. 'I love being alive,' she thought. 'Like my father I can't get over just being.'

The dog came in, cleaning its gums with a busy tongue. 'Who owns this place?' she asked it. 'Who's the girl with the cheap lipstick? I'm sure she doesn't live here—she was just a visitor.'

If she started digging herself out now perhaps she could be home for lunch. Light was beginning to caress the line of fat bellied pans arranged on a long shelf; one was dissolving in a small explosion of brightness. She pondered about the lipstick. If she were right and the girl had been disturbed while putting it on, where would the top be? In the bathroom, perhaps. She would look after breakfast—see if she was right. It wouldn't take a minute. She had all day to dig her way out of The Bield. Perhaps the sun would begin to soften the snow.

She licked the last of the yolk off the plate, because no one was there to see her and remind her that is wasn't manners. Even the dog had gone back to sleep.

The top of the lipstick wasn't in the bathroom; she found it on the bedroom floor. There didn't seem anything else out of place in the regimented loneliness of objects. It was a strange house, The Bield, she thought; even the things didn't seem ... at home. A house which couldn't encompass Aunt Mary's present from Teignmouth or mother's desperate, last-minute Christmas gift ... an aesthetic house, a ruthless house, a dead house. That was The Bield.

Her unease forced her downstairs. It was time she found a shovel: in a house with an open fire there was bound to be one. And yet curiosity had taken such a hold of her, she wanted to find out more about the farmhouse and its occupants. She could stay for another half-hour. Half-an-hour would make no difference. She had all day to work in.

The dog discovered her again and followed her into the lounge. It, too, began to sniff out the possibilities of the room.

She felt no guilt as she opened the drawer of the desk. The Bield owed her this after presenting her with the inexplicable, after filling her mind with all kinds of crazy terrors. Her long brown hair swept downwards to touch the private letters, the small, inward things collected· in them. The spelter clock raced through its delicate chimes to be followed by the flat-foot boom of the grandfather. She had no sense of the passing of her allotted half-hour. She was timeless now, caught up in the act of stealing into someone else's life.

3

The soft glow of gold caught her eye. The many-faceted Victorian locket she took into her hand reminded her of the one her grandma used to wear. She saw it lying on the slightly matted brown wool jumper. Grandma liked what she called 'practical' colours. Christie felt a tug towards a darkness she couldn't comprehend—or didn't want to comprehend?—some long, unspoken, unsung dusty pain. I don't want to know, she thought crossly; it's all gone and done with—finished. But people wouldn't be forgotten, would they? They lived on. They wouldn't be denied. They became part of the bio-chemical structure of the brain. They became part of you.

The locket slithered from her fingers and back into the drawer. So many years ago. There were so few to love, and of course you became cagey as you grew older and life got little too—little gossips, little enmities, little chores. And she would look out of her picture window on a blustery Saturday afternoon and wonder whether the brightness was lost for ever. Her grandmother had been so beautiful for those with eyes to see. She may have smelled of decay, her skeleton may have been bent by the rains of too many Northern summers, the draughts of too many winters; but her eyes had shone with a light as hurtfully young as the first sappy green of spring.

But what did it matter? The old woman was dead. She had been dead nine years. Why must she be haunted by shadows of what was and what might have been? Why must the past weigh the present? But it did. All the things undone, the love ungiven. It made the colours of the room sombre, it made her hand curl helplessly in her lap. The dog appeared at the door. 'Aren't you ever free?' The question was sharp. The dog slunk out again.

Oh dear, she thought. Have I ever felt so alone before?

She took out a bundle of photographs. There was a man in a peaked cap, his arms round a woman and another man. They were all laughing inanely. The woman had luscious long fair hair. She wore an unbecoming dress and thick lace-up shoes, an unlikely combination which seemed likely for her. She looked exciting, Christie thought, combustible. The third figure in the photograph seemed on the defensive, his hand partly covering his laughing face; a frizz of hair stood up on his head, making him taller than the others. There were Victorian photographs too, school photographs— faces of boys who must now be very old men or dead.

The dog decided to come in again. It was watching her, indecisive, wanting to be friendly but unwilling to be interrogated. She tried the cupboard under the drawer. It was locked. Should she force it open? That, surely, was the act of a vandal. She had no right to go through someone else's desk. What on earth possessed her?

She began to move restlessly about the room. Her grandmother wouldn't keep out of her thoughts. 'I don't normally think of her,' she despairingly told the dog. 'I never think of her.' She never cared to think of her; but here, in this place, in these alien surroundings, she seemed to breath in all the unbearable guilts.

'This is a terrible place. Something terrible has happened here.' She was convinced of it, and the sun came in through the farmhouse windows splintering dull solid objects into millions of dazzling fragments, laughing at all her apprehensions.

She sighed and spun from the sun.

'It's funny how it all ends,' she told the dog, 'how trivia eventually make you trivial—a caricature of what you were, what you are!' She and David had read *Wolf Solent* together, so long ago. It seemed inconceivable now that they had debated John Cowper Powys and his Place in the English Novel. Even the last time they had made love they afterwards talked of decorating the hallway and of how she wouldn't have to switch on the central-heating until afternoon at weekends and how she must make clothes on the secondhand machine he had bought for her birthday. 'I never thought of him as a practical man,' she confessed to the dog. The dog had settled on the rug and its enquiring presence had its own hard radiance. 'He can't seem to realise I'm not a practical woman. I'm a dreamer, a gazer at stars. The life he would have me lead will kill all of me. Like my father's and mother's situation, only in reverse,' she realised in horrified astonishment. And then she thought: 'Perhaps it will be all right if I wrap that bloody sewing machine round his neck!'

She began to move again, extremely agitated.

'Oh, if only there were someone in the barn! If it really had been a light from a torch I'd seen,' she told the dog, 'just someone else to talk to—another human being— how we would grin over my stupid fears. I'm getting out. I'm getting out of this place right now.'

She fetched a shovel from the kitchen. She opened the front door and surveyed her task. She felt helpless. I'll never do it, she thought, I'm trapped—trapped here. The light wind moaned in the sparkling unreal whiteness of that sparkling unreal morning. 'I can't do it. I can't get out.' Her sorrow seemed to meet and mingle with the low moan of the wind. Her breath hazed before her eyes, a visible manifestation of the implacable cold. Suddenly, viciously, she attacked the snow. She dug, dug, dug, dug at the ever-yielding, ever-soft whiteness. And then her work became more ordered and the trench she hewed became disciplined and properly proportioned.

Her limbs grew pleasantly tired and she glistened with sweat, steaming in the hard light.

'I feel so far away from everything I could be on another planet,' she thought.

What a pity she couldn't be like Miss Elizabeth Bennett and throw witty barbs at the world and be full of spirit. 'I am so exposed,' she thought. 'I feel so exposed that all I want to do is hide myself behind a grey exterior. An exterior as like everyone else's as I can possibly make it.'

She saw her role. Happy suburban housewife, never licking yolk off plates, making all her own clothes. A mass woman, a mass product, smashed into shape by the pressure of all the others. Suddenly she laughed at herself, and misthrown snow shook about her in icy delight. But what was she, who was she? 'What am I really like when I'm not trying so desperately hard to be like everyone else?' She wasn't a magician, like her father, and yet somehow she would have to come to terms with the fantastical streak in her nature, this flaw which threatened to bring her new semi-detached house about her ears in ruin, David with it.

Her work was slowing. The pleasant tiredness in her limbs had become a painful ache. 'But I've hardly made any headway—' She began to panic. 'I'll never get out!' Snow rained over her as she drove herself to frenzied effort. She stopped, panting, holding her side. 'Oh, the hell with it all,' she muttered. 'I'll have a cup of tea.'

She returned to the farmhouse. The dog stationed himself on the steps, watching with friendly interest. She glared at it as she went by. It whined.

There wasn't much left of the uneaten dinner she had found, but evidently the dog had no liking for brocolli, which lay quietly in an untouched white tureen. 'Perhaps I could wash the pots and put everything away.' Yet she felt uneasy about wiping out the last remains of the scene.

'Destroying the evidence.' Again she wondered. Evidence of what? There was the cut telephone wire too. And the dropped logs.

She hurried through the dining-room into the kitchen.

43

The house was much warmer, she realised: the central-heating must have switched itself back on. All these things, she thought, working away, not touched by God or man. She bustled with the tea. Her ankle was beginning to pain her again and she was glad to think of the chair she would soon sink into.

She would have liked to put sugar in her drink, but she was getting fat and she detected the self-indulgence this implied. Or did it imply something else entirely, she wondered, amused. How soon did a body with child begin to show that extra life? She had certainly been eating a lot recently: trifles, marmalade, sandwiches, rice puddings with thick, crushy skins, chips dipped in egg yolk—an orgy, really, of unbelievable delight. David too had noticed her growing curves and had infuriated her last week by calling her 'my Rubens'. She'd got her own back by saying: 'I'll really have to watch it. I'm getting just like my mother.' Her mother was thirteen stone, her face incomplete with plumpness—what should have been there half-hidden in flows of flesh. Grandma said that she had been the prettier of her two daughters, and even her mother sometimes spoke of the string of beaux she had had before she married. Perhaps the wrappers of plumpness had grown to protect a mutilated spirit. Now Christie knew only a woman whose gaze was often as barren as the winter hillside.

'He did for me,' she once told Christie, her head hidden behind a packet of breakfast cereal. 'Him and his magic! Pass the milk.' Christie understood but she couldn't find it in her to sympathise. Somehow she held her mother responsible for her father's sudden disappearance from their lives, for not having had the power to hold this man. He had blown through them like a breath of freedom, his presence speaking of distant marvels, of unseen skies of impossible hues, lands verdant beyond all comprehending. Yet he was a vulgar man, she conceded—his suits too sharp, his hair slicked

44

too neatly, a man with an eye for his own comforts and satisfactions.

She shut her eyes. His fingers looked so wide and clumsy, and yet how supple they were when he wove her a daisy chain—and then, good God, the daisies came out of his ears. He showed her how to suck the sap out of a stalk of grass and he wasn't afraid to paddle in a stream in winter or climb a tree with his best suit on. He never seemed to be aware that he might look foolish to others. He never seemed to notice that he wasn't a child any more.

She knew her father loved her. She had never doubted that, she didn't doubt it now. But when he ran off he never came back to see her. What kind of a love was that? It was a perpetual puzzle, a puzzle which she couldn't solve—perhaps never would.

She could hear the dog barking outside. She bit her fingers and listened to the nails tear. One day when she came home from primary school her mother took her up to her bedroom and told her that her father had 'gone with that Mrs Thatcher, silly bitch'. Her mother hadn't cried, hadn't looked distressed. Christie didn't believe her, not for a long time, but later she always took care to make sure where her mother was when she got home from school, marking her, as it were, present and correct. 'Our Chris is afraid I'll disappear in a puff o' smoke,' her mother told her cronies. And years afterwards Christie remembered the pain she felt as she turned the key in the front door, but her mother was always there, or somewhere near. 'I suppose that's what I resent so much, my horrifying dependence on her.'

The dog's barking was becoming frenzied.

Christie carefully set her cup on the saucer. The dog's noise now filled her mind. 'What is it?' she wondered. 'What's out there?' The sun-bright kitchen beamed back at her idiotically.

Reluctantly she got up and made her way through the

45

dining-room and down the hall. 'Shut up, dog. Quiet. Quiet.' She stood at the front door, hand shielding eyes against the firing marble of the sun.

The dog pushed past her, skittering to the far end of the trench she had dug, and began to leap up and down. Suddenly he threw back his head and yowled, a sound so urgent, so ancient, that Christie trembled before it. She moved to the left so she could see beyond the thick trunk of the oak. Beyond a curve in the snow, in front of the barn, another trench was being dug. The figure was small, compact, powerful, an exuberance of fizzing hair hiding his face.

Her heart leaped. A shout of joy was on her lips. But it never sang out of her. Her hand had unconsciously found her belly, as if guarding it, a keeper of the treasure which surely lay in there. 'Don't be stupid,' she muttered. 'This is what you've been waiting for, isn't it? Hoping. Someone to help you get out of The Bield, someone to talk to, just speak to—'

But she looked backwards into the dim hall, and her gaze found the cut telephone wire. 'This is really silly. Absolutely stupid. After all, he already knows that someone is here! He can see my trench. That I've been digging. Why don't I just run out? Meet him. Get it over with. How you'll laugh at yourself afterwards!'

And yet she couldn't quite bring herself to do it, she couldn't quite shake free from the nightmare The Bield had spun round her. Reluctantly she went into the lounge and sat on the sofa. She told herself that she needed time to think, to sort things out in her mind.

She arranged her hands neatly on her lap. She would rather be buried than burned. She wished she had told David that, but of course they had never discussed death. 'Not a spiritual flutter between us,' she murmured. 'Talking about it would be a dead end,' She giggled to herself. The sun, radiating off the windows, bathed her in its glow, and the pattern her rigid fingers made threw complicated shadows across her lap.

Rising, she moved quietly down the edges of the room, so that she couldn't be seen from the window, and placing herself in the shadow of curtain looked out towards the barn. The man worked with easy movements. The dog was quieter now but pawed at the snow and whined. Clearly the digger was his master. She watched the scene so intently and for so long that she felt the image of the digging man would never let her mind be free to conjure up future concepts. She wished again that she and David had discussed their dying. She didn't want her body to be burned; and burned it would be, shunted down that conveyor belt just like Grandma's. Earth: that was the rightful element, her element. Dust to dust. Slowly.

But why should the digging man harm her in any way? She didn't know him. He didn't know her. The dog was a stranger to the house, so his master must be too. Together they could get out of The Bield. Together they could be free. 'I wonder if he smokes,' she thought. 'I could do with a cigarette.'

Obviously he had got caught in the blizzard, just as she had, and had sought shelter in the barn. She stared at him again. He looked a very ordinary sort of man, in spite of his fizzing hair, not in the slightest bit alarming. Why, you wouldn't even notice him if he were next to you at a bus stop! He was wearing an anorak—rather like David's, now she came to think of it. She really must curb her imagination. She must go out of the farmhouse and meet him. Perhaps she could get some coffee ready for him.

But still she didn't move, more and more angry with herself. She shook herself, as if she could be rid of all unease, all apprehension. But alongside her fierce desire to make contact with the world again, to talk to the digging man, to share a joke with him, there was, too, this impulse to remain hidden away, out of harm's reach.

47

Her frustration grew. Well, she was going to have to meet him soon, wasn't she? What was the point in staying out of sight—cowering, yes, cowering, behind a curtain? If only she were home! Maureen, Dora, Juliette would be having a cup of coffee now, the children playing at their knees. Would they think she had run off with another man? They would enter and re-enter that topic with the singleminded dedication of bees sucking pollen. And yet she thought quite fondly of the three of them, grouped in a squabbling safety of life with broken washing machines and the vexed question of whether a child should be allowed to have a dummy.

There was her child, too—her own child to think of, the child she was sure was beginning to develop in her womb, the child that would soon lie in her arms.

Suddenly she got up and began to search about for a weapon. She picked up a brass candlestick and put it down. She caressed a heavy glass ash-tray. 'Things have got to be done proper.' Her grandmother's voice floated earnestly into her mind. 'Jaw tied up right and tight. It causes a lot o' grief, it does, a badly laid out loved one. The dead, poor souls, must have their due.'

Remembering the knife missing from the rack, she went into the kitchen. But a carving knife was surely ... well, to be taken seriously. If she chose a carving knife she would have to take her fears seriously. Perhaps a breadknife? But would it go in? It was so blunt-ended. There was the butcher's chopper, but that was too unwieldy. She began to laugh to herself. Lizzie Borden. Was that the name of the woman who committed such mayhem? Fingering one of the remaining carving knives, she set the electric sharpener to work. The sizzling steel took her sight away.

Of course, things would be easier if she could be sure that eternity was a figment of race imagination. That must be the most diabolical concept man ever invented. When she thought of the shades—of Grandma, for one—

the idea of life after death became monstrous. She was quite sure she had loved that old woman, but, by God, was she exasperating! Grandma made thoroughly unreasonable demands. Christie's relationship with her grandmother, she realised, had been fraught with guilt. She could never give enough to satisfy the old woman. With her father it had been different, but then he had taken to his heels with Mrs Thatcher. 'And she won't give him no basin of black peas ...' her mother had announced with satisfaction. Christie remembered her father, fork in hand, attacking a pound or more, never talking, never pausing from shovelling them into his mouth: a man of great appetites, great energies, and yet a man, too, who was given to mind-stopping idleness. Her mother had poked at that idleness like a witch with a pitchfork. 'Cut the lawn, cut the lawn!' At last he roared with a great yell of pain and went out and sprinkled paraffin over the grass. He put a match to it and burned his arm in the sheets of flame. Her mother thrust his injury under the cold tap and listened stony-faced to his howls of agony. Christie watched from under the table, childish eyes round and fascinated and yet her body strung-up and fearful, hoping the world above would not collapse upon her. No, no. No, no. She didn't want to meet any shades that had gone before her or those to be thrust down the dark hole after her. The only mercy was complete annihilation, an end to all that had been and was no more.

She weighed the knife in her hand. Fire split through the steel, explosion after explosion. The weapon was heavy in her hand, but in her eye it was a magical, mysterious, ever-changing entity.

She went to the window and stood against the shadow of the curtain. The man was now resting on his spade, a lighted cigarette in his mouth, his eyes on the moorland skyline above the farmhouse. She felt rather foolish as she looked at the knife in her hand. Why, after all, would he want to do her harm? He was just a benighted traveller, like her.

She turned to face the alien room. At the back of her mind she was wondering whether James I of England was James VI of Scotland. The answer to the question seemed so important that she felt a great pain in her head, and then her mind began to spiral slowly round and she felt that if she got to the bottom of the spiral she would be mad. 'Madness wouldn't help,' she told the bird skeletons. She moved restlessly about, her long, dark hair swinging on the air. The hair, her hands, her toes, felt frayed as though her extremities were disintegrating under some intolerable central friction.

She was back at the window. He was digging again. He had another fifteen feet of snow to shift, she calculated, before his trench reached hers. What then?

Why hadn't David stopped her from running out of the house? He had stood at the door of their semi-detached like a great wounded bear, made impotent by her anger.

'Marriage has nothing to do with love,' her grandmother had warned her. 'Passion is killed soon enough. It's a knack. That's what it is. Marriage is a knack.' The flames from the fire had leapt up the walls, sometimes thrusting 'Highland cattle Grazing' into the light, sometimes shrouding the picture in implacable dark. 'Marriage is short commons. Marriage is doing things you don't like, doing and lumping it. Marriage is giving in.' Grandma spoke with ever-increasing doleful relish, but the girl, warmed by the magic fire, the squeaky armchair pulled in toastingly close, was more aware of the charmed circle to which she belonged than her grandmother's voice. She remembered how the old woman's perfectly round spectacles glinted and how withered her face was in outline, like a November rose. Christie used the tongs to put a fallen red-hot coal back into the grate. 'But you loved grandfather?' 'That came

50

later.' 'Later?' 'When we'd knocked the spots off each other. Then he went and died. Silly old bastard.' And that was the one thing her grandmother could not forgive— his death.

Christie put the knife down, suddenly afraid of it. The blade must be a foot long, she guessed. Did she really think she could use it on a man? They would laugh about this, she thought, in relief, she and that digging man. They would laugh about her crazy notions. But she picked up the knife again, selecting an orange from the bowl of fruit and slicing through it. The knife was so sharp. She watched the juice from the orange run out into the wooden bowl, dipping her finger in it and tasting it, and screwing up her face. Oh Jesus, Jesus, what must I do? The dog was barking again—frantic, urgent yowls. He must have almost cut through to her.

She broke and raced out of the room, up the stairs, and stopped on the landing, looking left and right. Suddenly she spun round, the dog's wild joy driving her forward, and plunged into a bedroom. She opened a wardrobe door and bundled herself in, snapping the door shut and blinking in the gloom. Her heart was boxing her ears.

'You're a fool,' came the acid comment from the cool of her soul. 'You're ridiculous, sitting in a wardrobe in broad daylight. He got caught in the blizzard just like you and dug his way out of the barn for food. And to have company. Your company. He was alone. Lonely. Just like you.'

Distractedly she wove a piece of her long hair through her lips and bit on it. When she was small and frightened she had clutched at her mother's leg and her mother had laughed and put up with it. She looked down at the knife, which lay quietly in her hands, glinting, insubstantial, like water. 'Go out. Face him,' reason told her.

In the hall below her she heard the crunch of feet and the dog's short, exultant trills. Well, he was in the house. This man. 'What now?' she asked herself crossly. 'I can't live in a wardrobe. It's quite ridiculous, a grown woman cowering in a wardrobe. You're ridiculous. You're absurd. Why should he harm you?'

She eased cramped feet. 'Anyway, if he really did kill you where would he put you? The ground is too frozen to dig a grave. And if you stick this knife in him, where will you put him?' 'In the loft,' came the surprising answer. 'People never go in lofts for years on end. A dark, far corner, under the fibre glass insulation.' She frowned. But wouldn't the smell of his deadness, his rotting, penetrate into the rooms below? She moved uneasily. Oh Christ. Oh for home and the two-bar electric fire and the coldness of the central heating radiators turned down for economy! 'But it will certainly be a good selling point, a good selling point in a house,' had been David's earnest assurance. Oh for a cigarette, and tea, a cup of tea ... and ordinariness. It was all out there, beyond the wardrobe, surely all out there somewhere.

She brushed away the self-pitying tears and tried to make herself more comfortable. Rough wool and the smell of dry cleaning. And it was so cramped in here, such an ache, like having flu and thinking one was dying. 'I don't want aspirins, woman,' said her father, sweating in bed. His voice was crusty with northern vowel-sounds like skin that was chapped. 'Whisky, whisky!' And growing dramatic: 'Whisky to drown the buggers in!' 'Can't drown bits o' flu virus. Can't be done. Won't get 'erselves drowned. Any fool knows that.' Four aspirins appeared in the smashed rock of her mother's hand. He had gazed at his wife in impotent fury. She grinned, a ragged, half-triumphant grin, and produced a glass of whisky to wash them down with. 'Daft that's what you are,' she told him roundly. 'Loose in th' 'ead,' 'I 'urt, you 'ard-faced besum. I 'urt. I bloody well 'urt. All bloody well over.' He was almost in tears. 'Keep yer out o' mischief then, won't it? For a while,' came the reply, and her mother's face was a thousand rainy Sundays.

Christie tried shuffling her aching limbs. She shouldn't be here. She had no place in a wardrobe. What was she doing in a wardrobe? She began to feel thoroughly confused.

Did she really expect someone to walk up the stairs and kill her? Of course she didn't. She must see reason. Did any of her friends sit in wardrobes waiting to be killed? They didn't. There was a name for it. She was paranoid, that was it.

She heard footsteps on the stairs. Her hand went upwards to protect her neck. So vulnerable. Such an easily getatable part of one's body. In her mind's eye was the neat cut across the cream telephone wire. If he had used the knife missing from the rack to cut the wire, he would surely still have it on him. She heard a door open. The door to the room in which she was hiding? She stuffed a fist into her mouth. A tap was running. Her bones slackened. He was across the landing. She could stay in the wardrobe all day and then she could creep out of the house when he was asleep at night. But where would she go? The snow imprisoned as implacably as bars. There was the barn. Musical chairs. Oh dear, Oh dear. Was survival worth all this?

She moved cramped arms. A coat-hanger crashed against the back of the wardrobe. Her fright exploded in a little hiss of air. Her mind went out again, beyond the wardrobe, searching for his presence. The tap continued to run. When you lay in the sea and turned up your belly to soak up its sun, you knew all about the necessity for being alive. Perhaps she would go to the sea again some day. To her mother the elements were a nuisance, something to be borne without silence; even God was a nuisance, who on no account must stop her pegging out her clothes, or hoovering or visiting bingo at four o'clock ... Muffins for tea, toasted by her mother on the coal fire, and butter running down the sides of their mouths and their eyes winking at each other … would the world ever taste as good again?

Her head began to fall towards rough, tweed slacks. It was so hot in the wardrobe. She was fainting. Through fear? Or lack of air? She was confused. The trouble was, her thighs were too fat. She must give up eating muffins. She must tell her mother not to get any more muffins. They were so tempting. She wouldn't be able to wear a bikini if she kept stuffing down the muffins. Hot, hot beach … too hot. And her head buried itself in the embrace of tweed.

Barking grew as big as trees in her head, a wood, a forest, an obliteration of well-being. She opened her eyes, born again. The light was so white, so frightening. Nowhere: nowhere to go, to hide. Her hand blindly reached to shut the wardrobe door.

The sock, red and thick and pungent. Man smell. His sock. The green corduroy leg, the thick cream sweater, the steel rim of spectacle. Sepia eye.

'Hello,' he said.

The dog licked her leg.

'Oh, hello,' she said. She wondered what to do with the knife, still in her hand. She began to grin at him foolishly.

'You were asleep.'

'Yes.' How could she admit that she had fainted with fright?

'Can I help you?'

'Help me?'

'Out.'

'Oh. Oh, yes.'

They both fell to studying the knife, wondering what to do for the best.

'It seems a strange thing to carry around,' he hazarded cautiously. 'It must be very sharp.'

'Yes.' And she added quickly: 'Very good with oranges. For cutting them, I mean. Very good for that.'

'I don't think a wardrobe can be a very comfortable

place.' He offered her an arm to help her out. She took it, and the pain from her injured ankle made her bite her lip.

'Are you hurt?'

She surveyed him, and relief began to flood through her. He was concerned: concerned about her, about her injury. He was certainly a bit odd-looking, but he seemed friendly, innocuous ...

'Just twisted my ankle a bit. Nothing, nothing at all.' His brown hair sprouted in glorious clumps and fell shaggily about his brow and shoulders. He looked, she thought, like an up-dated Jesus Christ in glasses, except he wore corduroy trousers which were too big when he should be in skin-tight jeans. And wasn't there something vaguely familiar, something recognisable, about his stance? Hadn't she seen him before somewhere?

She realised he was studying her as intently as she was studying him. His broad hands rested lightly on his hips. 'Do you always sleep in wardrobes?' His voice was soft and there was an undertone she had difficulty in deciphering. Laughter? He was laughing at her.

She was beginning to feel very embarrassed. What on earth could she do with the knife. Heat rushed to her cheeks. She was blushing. Would he notice if she dropped the weapon on the bed behind her? It was awkward in her hand, ridiculous, large and, yes—obscene. She suppressed a giggle.

'I've started making some lunch for you.'

'How did you know I was here?'

'Well, there was that trench you dug,' he reminded her, drily, 'Not to mention your bits and pieces. All over the house. Your clothes are still drying in the bathroom.'

He led the way downstairs, and she followed him timidly. She found it difficult to discard the knife: the damned thing seemed riven to her—aching, uncomfortable, still carrying all her terror in its shimmering, murderous confines.

4

He had made cheese on toast. She tried to avoid acknowledging him, but she was almost constantly aware of the sun glinting on his steel-rimmed glasses. A mythical beast, she thought, with swords of light piercing his brow. She was so nervous that molecules of her being seemed in perpetual, dizzying motion. When they had entered the kitchen he had turned to her and gingerly taken the knife from her, his fingers on the steel, his body tight with unspoken excitement. He had hung the knife back on the hook. It lay there now—out of the light, rendered dull, powerless. Her unarming had left her chillingly exposed.

The meal was eaten in silence, the instruments rattling politely, salt and pepper moving about in a ritual of propitiation. At length it came to her that the silence was being laboriously created, spinning slowly round and round them, binding them together in a cocoon of unending conspiracy, a secret at the centre of many secrets.

'You were expecting to use it?'

She started. The broken quiet caught her so unawares that she found she was shouting a frightened 'What?'.

'The knife.' He measured sugar into his tea. His hands were stubby and powerful. Hair curled thickly on their backs.

Almost surprised, she said, 'You didn't attack me.'

'Ah, you were expecting to be attacked? You were expecting me to attack you? That accounts for it.'

She stared across the chasm between them, feeling its coldness, its nuances of terror, and in the unending reflection of pots apprehended her mortality. 'Someone cut the telephone wire. It frightened me.'

'Yes. I did notice that. It wasn't you?'

'Me?'

'I wondered, perhaps, if you were running away from something, someone ...'

'Why on earth would I disconnect the telephone? Besides, I'm not running away from anything!' She felt confused, not quite knowing what to say to him, but it seemed important to keep the conversation going, to maintain contact. She said: 'Running away won't do. Cowardly.' She stopped short, aware how foolish she sounded. He had, after all, just found her hiding in the wardrobe upstairs. She blushed.

He didn't answer. She didn't dare look to see whether he was laughing at her.

On she plunged 'One had better stick to one's ground and fight.' It was amazing how clearly she saw this now. It was as if, in the last few years, she had ceased to believe in free will, and so it was taken from her and she had lain enslaved in a mesh of her own creating.

'Ah. I see.' He was mocking her. 'A fighter after all!'

She was unsure. 'Who knows?'

'So you didn't cut the telephone wire?'

'No,' she attacked. 'Did you?'

He was laughing out loud now. 'Why should I do that?'

If only she could see his eyes, she thought. If only he didn't wear those glasses. She couldn't begin to gauge his character. She was frightened of him, sometimes heart-stoppingly so, but he excited her too. The strength in his hands excited her, his strangeness, the cold smell of his unimaginable night in the barn. And there was something vaguely familiar about him. 'I don't know. I don't know why you should cut the telephone wire.' And then, abruptly: 'The people aren't here. Did you know them?'

He took a long time to consider the matter. 'No.'

But wasn't he the taller of the two men in the photograph she had seen when she rifled the desk? She became outraged. 'You're lying!'

He didn't answer. He began to study her and though he was still sitting and apparently at ease she became aware that his body was growing more aggressive. 'What a pity—'

'What?'

'A shame. To be caught in the storm. A nuisance.'

Suddenly she saw herself as he had been seeing her, small and pale, long hair hiding mobile unformed features; and in her very seeing she felt her face harden, felt the iron being created in her soul hone away layers of uncertainty to come to ... what? 'I expect you must endure,' she said; and as she became aware of his astonishment she added apologetically: 'I expect you must endure these things.'

'My God, you sound like Old Mother Time!' he said, and then added thoughtfully: 'You might have used that knife.'

She had an intimation that she could, indeed, reach out and take power, invest power in herself. 'Perhaps. Yes. Perhaps.'

He was exultant. 'And you were such a mouse. Screwed up and scared in that wardrobe.'

'Extreme situations ... I mean, one could act in a bizarre way, out of character.'

'No one ever acts out of character. Extreme situations can only compress one into the quintessence of self.'

'You have thought about it?'

'I am a thoughtful man,' he said composedly. 'And you?'

'I haven't tended to think, only to be pushed back and forward in thought, like a rudderless ship.' She looked up quickly, aware of exposing a weakness in herself and yet needing to mirror herself in him, so that she could see her reflection and then ... and then ... know? Just that? Be? Change?

Abruptly she changed the subject. 'Something happened here. Something horrible. Not only the telephone wire.' She told him about the uneaten meal, the upturned chair.

He rose while she was talking and moved about, his back turned towards her, so that she couldn't surmise whether he was impatient because she told him what he already knew or whether what she told him made him uneasy?

'I gave most of the meal to your dog,' she finished. 'I couldn't bear the sight of it.'

'Why?'

'Spooky. I—'

'What?'

'Awful. Something awful has happened.'

'Have you any proof? Is this just fanciful speculation?'

'No proof.'

'What do you think happened, my dear?'

He had turned towards her. His hair swung gently about his shoulders. It was shining, well-kept. A vain man, she thought. Does he consciously cultivate the Jesus look? Perhaps he thinks that looking like God is part way to becoming godlike.

He was irritated by her long silence. 'Well?'

'Something odd happened. We ought to look into it! Do you know who lived here? You do, don't you?'

'Yes. Of course.'

She sighed. 'Well, I mean. What about him? Was he queer?'

He grinned. 'What makes you think that?'

She considered. 'The way the meal was laid out. The way things, small things ... the way they were arranged in patterns. Oppressive patterns.'

'My God.' He was disgusted. 'A man is queer, is he—a man is queer just because he has an eye for design?'

'Well, was he?'

'Is he, don't you mean? You will have to stop being so dramatic. You are—' he paused to choose his words with care '—trying to give substance to what are only fantasies. Your—'

'Terrors. Perhaps. Being alone in this place so long. The idea in your head becomes the reality. You project something and no one is there to give the lie to it. To refute it. I—No!'

'No?'

'I don't care what you say. How you try to diminish it. Something happened. I feel it in my bones.'

'Don't be ridiculous.'

'Horror. An intimation of horror—'

'Nothing happened. Nothing at all. If something had, it would be obvious ... It—'

'He isn't queer then?' she cut across him. 'The man who lived—lives here?'

'Of course not!'

'Who is he then?'

'Head of the art college. Dermott.'

'But why did you lie about it? It's so silly!'

'Questions ... questions. It's bloody boring, that's why.' He moved fretfully.

'He lives here alone?'

'He's not a hermit, if that's what you mean.'

'What—'

'He has friends.'

'Mistresses?'

'How you sound when you say that word! Like a nun in a cold bath. I don't know about a permissive society— you women up north are still often Baptist round the edges. I expect so. Yes. I don't know him that well!' He pointed a finger at her. 'You. What about you? Are you married?'

'Yes. This Dermott—were you visiting him last night?'

He turned and leaned against the kitchen sink. The harassed look had left his face. He lit a cigarette with such precision of movement that she wondered whether some inner will had controlled and calmed him. 'Not really.'

'What does that mean?' she exploded.

'I was on my way to the pub—to Owd Bett's. The bike went off the road, the dog escaped from the sidecar and by the time I'd stopped looking for him I was aware of the hell of a mess I was in. Snow up to my thighs. The wind knocking the innards out of me. Frozen stiff. I thought I'd get up to the farmhouse, but I only managed to reach the barn.'

She felt he wasn't telling her the truth, and she tried to control her growing frustration. 'Why did you say you didn't know who lived here?'

'I'm what's known as a slippery character,' he informed her blithely. 'Invention often makes life fun. I invent edifices if I please. Huge edifices of fantasy.'

'You're a liar!' she shouted.

'Yes!' he yelled 'And so are you! Bodies in cupboards! Whoever heard anything so daft!'

They were staring furiously at each other. The anger went out of his face and she gradually became aware of his pain, a great open wound of a face, a destruction which couldn't be hidden behind steel-rimmed spectacles. 'Shall we open cupboards and look?' he taunted.

'Look?'

'To see if your imagination has body ...' He began to laugh. The pain was packed so tightly away again that she began to wonder if she had imagined it.

'I don't know your name,' she said abruptly.

'Lionel. I'm not called that, though. I'm called Leo.'

'Who calls you Leo?'

'My friends.' He smiled. 'In my thoughts, too, I call myself Leo. One's name is, after all, a serious matter.

61

How one projects oneself is very important, don't you think?'

'You've obviously thought a lot about it.'

'Of course. But not you. I remember now. The rudderless ship. It really won't do, my dear. It behoves you to be objective.'

'To survive?' she asked sharply.

'That was my theory. Those who are invaded, those who aren't. But unfortunately it's all a lot more subtle than that. My mother's a timid, grey little creature who's always going back to make sure she has turned off the gas, locked the door. But she invades us all, she still does, like the sea. My father and I have always been caught up in the forces of her inconsistencies. Now, are we going on that body hunt or aren't we?'

'Are you married?'

'The second time around. Jane.'

'What happened to the first?'

'She died. And before your imagination gets to work I'll tell you that it was legitimate. That's if you can regard suicide as legitimate.'

'Do you?'

'She was as daft as a brush,' he said shortly.

Christie was aware of delicately treading on fractured ground, but she persisted. 'Why did you marry her then?'

'I like imperfect women! The chipped vessel, the crazed soul … How the hell do I know! Really know! Why did you marry your husband?'

'Can I have a cigarette?'

He gave her one. 'She was older than me—quite a bit older, as a matter of fact. God knows why we choose as we do. I don't know the needs in me which a woman, a wife, must fulfil. Needs are so often hidden. We aren't aware of them. I wish I did know. Understand. Knock, and it shall be opened. Oh, but that's the Bible. I was going to be a priest once, a holy man.'

62

She stared at him, thinking, but not sure, that this was more of his inventions. 'What happened?' she asked ironically.

He was grim. 'It was the image—the idea—don't you see? The ritual of the altar. The sign of the cross, the black robes, the mystery. It was the picture.'

As he spoke she saw his picture, its sombre patterns shockingly shot through with stained-glass light. 'Do you have a match? A light? For my cigarette.'

He bent towards her. His hand momentarily touched hers as he lit her cigarette. The contact sent a small shock wave through her. She looked at him. Their eyes smiled at each other.

She drew back quickly. 'It didn't happen, though.'

'Of course not!' He grinned. 'It was the doctrine. Turning the other cheek and all that. What a boring thing to do. What a negative thing. It's against life. No. It was just the picture. That's what fascinated me.'

'You aren't a holy man.'

'Couldn't refine myself. Didn't want to refine myself. I just wanted to be. But what, I'd no idea! Well, shall we go on this body hunt then?' He was suddenly brisk. 'That would be good fun. I've never been on one before.' He opened a kitchen cupboard and began to root through it. 'There should be a torch about somewhere. Ah, just the thing. Adds a nice touch, don't you think? A body hunt just wouldn't be the same without a torch. There's a cellar. This house does have a cellar. Have you been down it?'

She shook her head.

'You've got too much hair,' he complained. 'I can't see you—know what you're thinking.'

'Does it matter? You obviously don't take what I think seriously.'

'But do you? Do you really?'

'Yes. Oh, I don't know. I expect it does sound ridiculous. Only ... I don't know. The cut telephone wire.

I mean, you've seen that!'

'Yes,' he conceded. 'That's odd. That gives some spice to the search.'

She felt him move closer to her again, but she didn't look up. She couldn't quite bring herself to acknowledge his presence.

He mused: 'You know, I can't quite put my finger on you yet. You seemed such a scared little thing. Submissive. But now I'm not so sure. Even when I see your face it doesn't stay still, the same.'

'Don't be ridiculous. You—'

'No. I can't say you're like this ... or that ... You seem to change all the time ... a spring landscape—'

'Protective colouring.' She wasn't unpleased by his nonsense. It had been a long time since anyone had looked at her, tried to find out what she was like. She felt it had been a long, long time. She wondered about his hands on her, touching, undressing her. Her fingers uncurled, moving slightly out towards him, and yet she was afraid of him too. She turned in confusion.

He, too, had moved further from her. 'Are you coming with me? To the cellar?'

'What?' Her voice was sharp.

'The body hunt.'

'All right.' But she was reluctant.

'We'll find something?'

'How do I know!'

'I'll go first.'

She followed him, keeping a measured, arm's-length distance from his body. 'You don't come from these parts.' She was trying to make some sense of him, the contradictions in her feelings towards him. But her fear of him and the powerful attraction he had for her seemed to be one and the same—couldn't be separated out, one from the other. 'You aren't from here.'

'From the south. I came up last year.' He slowed to light a cigarette. She came to an abrupt half behind him.

My God, she thought despairingly. Where does my imagination end and he really begin? 'I expect it's hard. Hard for you to settle. It's a bit grim. The town ...' Oh yes ... the lush grass bending under her feet and the balmy breezes of many springs—breezes punting an old mattress down the canal—and the nearly hidden harebells gleaming under the patch of elderberries which fringed a howling townscape.

'Sometimes it's like seeing through fungus,' he said. 'Grey fungus. But it clears, and the images bite into the backbone.' He smiled suddenly. 'And, of course, the people tend to savage those not like themselves. For instance ... how they hate the word "one". Queer. Pouf. One mustn't say this, one mustn't do that, especially one must never use the word "oneself".'

'But naturally, you use the word "one" all the time,' she hazarded.

'Naturally. When one's staked out one's territory, my dear, one doesn't budge an inch. It's here. Under the stairs.' He opened the cellar door.

The coldness from below seeped upwards and stirred in eddies about the warm hall.

Christie was shivering. 'I wonder if there's a light.'

'Well, he had this place converted. Dermott. Open-tread stairs, pine galley kitchen ...' The great black mouth of the cellar drew their eyes, their minds. It suddenly bounded into light. 'There. Don't break your neck on the steps. They're steep.'

'I'll take every care.'

'You're priceless!' He turned and swept her hair away from her face, studying her intently, impersonally. She remained very still but very hidden, her awareness slipping deeper and deeper into herself. He put the torch into his pocket and began to descend the stairs. 'I saw you up there in the wardrobe, curled up and twitchy and I thought, Ah! mouse-like. But you're cat-like. My God, you are!'

65

'A painter. I ought to have realised. But, you know, even bank clerks are all artistic and hairy these days.'

'Head of Fine Art. Dermott was my boss.'

'Was?' she yelped.

'Dear, dear. You've got me at it now. Is. Is my boss.'

They came down into the cellar, the air icily round them, so that now when they spoke small clouds ballooned about them—grey, dissipating haloes of gas, slowly circling the stone flags and each other like figures in a pagan dance.

Christie said: 'There's a small cellar off. Look in there.'

'All right.' He turned on the torch.

She moved nearer him, but at the last minute checked herself, her excitement at fever-pitch but its underpinning terror making her cautious. The beam moved through lonely blackness and then illuminated a bulging sack, ranging over the sack, the floor and slowly up her to her face. She was transfixed in the light. 'What's your name? I don't even know that?'

She spun out of the beam. 'Christie.'

'Not Christine? Have you indulged in a little image-making too? No, no. I don't believe that. You don't project well ... confused ... a confused pattern.'

'My father. My father did it. He took the "n" out. To make it magic—that's what he said.'

'Magic?'

'He was a magician. He made magic.' She was suddenly laughing. 'He was quite famous for his disappearing act.'

'Shall I look in the sack? It will only be neatly bundled rubbish; though. Dermott was tidy, body-and-soul a tidy man. And that doesn't make him queer! The men in the north must have a hard time of it ... being louts to prove their manhood.'

He had bent down and was already untying the sack. Christie was retreating. We might be a million miles from the sun, she thought, down here, down in this cellar. And she felt the icy dampness permeating her bones, uniting her with the stones about her.

A shower of bright sugar papers floated on to the floor, their garish colours scattering on the flags like a fair on waste ground.

'That's how he works,' Leo said. 'He shuffles his sugar-paper shapes about on the board until he has it right. Then he knocks them off. Two or three days later he starts to paint. Something happens to those shapes in his mind. They become ... ominous. Southerners like being frightened. His last exhibition was a sell-out.'

'People bought his paintings?' Christie was impressed. Like many in the town, she was cynical about art. If you had a good pair of eyes, what did you need a picture for? Eyes were cheaper, better, and could be more devious in their reaction to light.

'Not that he needs money,' Leo went on. 'His father had the good sense to manufacture boiled sweets and then get swallowed by a bigger concern ... for a consideration of course.' Leo stopped to seek the right words. 'He—expects everything and gets it!' He laughed. 'More than he bargained for.'

'There's something at the bottom of the sack,' she said. 'Something more.'

Leo delved again and took out some magazines. 'Girlie things. His shapes may have been abstract but they had passionate beginnings.'

There was something hard, aggressive, in his voice, she thought, and she realised he didn't like Dermott.

He was stuffing everything back in the sack. 'Must be tidy.' His voice was mocking. 'Tidiness is a sign of a disciplined mind and a disciplined mind is in full control of itself and its environment.'

'That's what Dermott thought?'

'Yes.'

'Do you believe that?'

'When I have the energy. It takes a lot of energy.'

The feeling of inadequacy which often destroyed her

ability to sustain independent thought swamped her. 'I'm a muddler. A stumbler.'

'That's what I thought when I saw you first, up in the bedroom. Controlled by things, events, everything but yourself. Dermott decided he was king and so he is: king of his little world.' He was briskly refastening the neck of the sack. 'One can admire a man like that.'

'Can one?' she mocked.

Sharply he booted the sack back into the second cellar. 'Well, shall we continue our hunt, my dear?'

She was already on the cellar steps, determined to reach the safety of the hall quickly. She didn't think he would lock her in the cellar, indeed why should he? There's no harm in being sure, she assured herself, as she winged up the flight of steps. She winced as a sharp pain shot up from her ankle. His presence behind her black and potent, and layered with intricate messages, intricate secrets, was filling her imagination. The strange thing was that as this man took an ever stronger hold on her the figure of her husband stirred to life again: distant, but quiet and reassuring. A map reference, a guide to home territory.

The hall was warm and lapped in trickles of light. She spun round it, glad to be free. Free of what? The cellar which had proved empty of bodies?

Leo put out the light. He banged the door shut on the gaping blackness.

'There's a broom cupboard under the stairs.' His voice was reckless, gay even. 'Shall we look at the brooms?' But as they faced each other his sudden exhilaration drained away, and the distance between them was tinged by a despair which grew from a half-apprehended feeling that they were the unwilling victims of a tragic game.

She lifted up her head. 'Open the door then. Open the cupboard door.'

'By the way, your clothes ought to be dry now. I put them on a radiator.'

'How thoughtful.'

His words were sharp. 'You can't keep wearing that man's clothes.'

'Does it distress you? Does it distress you, Leo?'

'They're too big. Eating was his Achilles' heel.'

Stepping forward she wrenched open the cupboard door and quickly backed away so that it could swing back. They stared at the preternatural neatness of brushes, vacuum cleaner, polishes.

'Don't you think this charade ought to stop?' he said. 'I really think I've indulged your fancies enough, my dear.'

'What's that?' The long finger pointed to the back of the cupboard.

'What?'

'That cloth. Bring it out.'

He took a brush and swept the cloth towards her in a savage but controlled stroke. It hit her feet, and she picked it up.

'I wouldn't have noticed it, but it wasn't in its proper place. It wasn't part of the pattern.' She held it out. 'I think it's blood. I think it's been used to mop up blood.' She dropped it quickly.

He used the brush to hook it towards him. 'Yes.' The grandfather clock moved into its hourly strokes, which reverberated with time, and they were then set loose, figures in a dream landscape.

Suddenly he hurled the brush back into the cupboard and slammed the door. The wood quivered with his fury. She watched him through narrowed eyes, fingers curled, claw-like.

He became aware of her by degrees as he controlled his anger. The steel-rimmed spectacles burned with opaque light. 'Well?' was all he said.

Had he, she wondered, precipitated this crisis? Was he driving something to its conclusion? When she tried to walk her steps were unsteady, and she kept her sick fear well away from the surface of her mind, the surface of her face. Her walk strengthened. Instinctively she felt that she mustn't show weakness, that he would take advantage of weakness. And it seemed to her that her will was growing all the time. He wouldn't find her easy to harm. Out of the window, wedges of white were appearing in the iced blue sky. The sun went in.

'What have you come into the dining-room for?' He had moved up behind her.

Goosepimples stirred, mouse quiet, on her skin. 'There was a stain on the table cloth. I thought it might have been a wine stain. There.' She showed him the mark, near where the wheel-backed chair had been turned over.

Reluctantly he bent to examine it. 'Well, I don't know. It could be anything. This one could. No smell.'

'Not as much. Not as much blood.' She was on her knees examining the multi-striped rug.

He turned his head so that he could see her better.

She said: 'I don't know how I missed it. Of course, the pattern on the rug is very bright. And last night there was only artificial light.' She stood up, her feet marking but not intruding upon the stain. 'Someone made a good job of cleaning it up. If I hadn't looked for it, I would probably never have noticed.'

'What do you think happened?' he asked.

She began to realise that as each small piece of evidence came to light the need to reach conclusions became more urgent. And those conclusions might be fatal for her. Her fright was now a perceptible thing, something she could no longer hide. She leaned on the table for support.

'What do you think happened?' He was becoming aggressive.

'I don't know!'

'What's this all about then?'

'I don't know.'

'You—'

She felt desperate. 'Perhaps your friend Dermott had

70

an accident. Perhaps that's why he's not here. Whoever was with him took him to hospital.'

'No bodies?' he barked.

'There aren't any, are there!'

'No,' he sighed. 'No, my dear.'

She realised for the first time that though his clothes, his hair, his style, were flamboyantly young, he was not. At first she had thought him in his twenties, but now something in the tone of his voice, something in the way the lines gathered on his face when he let his tension melt, pointed to the mid-thirties.

'Dermott won't like it,' he said suddenly.

'What?'

'The stain on the rug. Dermott is very particular. He's always on about the purity of line. "That's the essence," he'd say. "The only positive statement." I'm not very keen on all this shape business. All this revealing. There's a lot to be said for deviousness. Suggestions of this and that. Artistically speaking, of course.'

She had the impression that though he was ostensibly talking to her he was, in fact, communing with himself. 'I don't know about art,' she said abruptly. 'I don't know about artists. I've never thought about it.'

'Well, you naturally wouldn't have anything to do with it.' He seemed surprised she should even have to state her position.

'Why not?'

'He was a magician, wasn't he? Your father?'

She was bewildered. 'What on earth has that to do with it? What are you talking about?'

'Magicians—people like you—never make images of themselves. Dissipation of power. Besides, an image might be used against them.'

'My father was a children's conjuror! Not—not ... nothing to do with witchcraft, black magic.'

'The branch is part of the same tree. And you're of the inheritance.'

71

'What a crazy idea! What a silly notion. Ridiculous.'
But she was shocked to find that the small surge of power
in her was so familiar—not so much something in her
memory as a race remembrance. She had an
extraordinary feeling that one more push and her mind
would run over time and move backwards and forwards
into knowledge.

They had left the dining-room and had gone into the
lounge, not one following the other but both acting on a
collusion of impulse. The dog got up and stretched itself.
It didn't seem to know which of the two to go to, so it just
wagged its tail and sat down again. The sun suddenly
flooded the house and they blinked.

'No bodies.' Christie smiled.

'No.' And he smiled too.

It was as if they had both agreed to sweep facts and
fears under the carpet, at least for now, while the sun
shone and the dog wagged its tail and the day came to its
zenith.

5

She had ironed her slacks and was wearing them. She had stowed Dermott's clothes away neatly and bandaged her ankle again. It was still swollen, still sore, but the tight wet bandages supported it well. Now, placidly, she sat in front of the dressing-table mirror combing her hair. A dreadful dullness had fallen on the afternoon, making the objects leaden, making her moving image leaden too. Colour had trickled out of the room, trickled out of her, leaving a stoically despairing landscape.

Before Leo had gone to sleep, before she had been exasperated by the sound of his snoring and the sight of his sleep-silly face, which resembled nothing so much as melting wax, he had told her: 'Clara was a schizophrenic.'

'Who's Clara?'

'My first wife.'

'Didn't you know before you married her?' The trouble with Leo was you didn't know when truth ended and fabrication began. Or did truth ever begin?

'I suppose I did. In a way.'

'What do you mean?'

'Well, I knew her, didn't I? I thought she was flamboyant. She excited me in such a way. Like an abstract. Like one of Dermott's abstracts.'

'She killed herself, didn't she? How did she do it?'

'Nothing messy. She took an overdose. I found her one morning.'

'What did you do?'

'Do?' He gave a sudden bark of laughter. 'The dead are dead, dear.' He got up and put the television on. The gliding, yattering fingers filled the small screen. He retreated to his chair.

'You married again.'

He didn't answer her directly. He said: 'This one is lame. I appear to like my women ... incomplete. Perhaps I feel I've more of a fighting chance if they have, metaphorically speaking, one arm tied behind their backs.' Almost as an after-thought, he added: 'But you are whole.'

She paused in the laborious brushing of her hair. Was he classing her among 'my women'? She felt indignant. He was a fraud. Thirty aping twenty. A liar, an inadequate. She had to admit, though, he stirred her sexually. But she didn't respond to his unthought demand in a submissive way. Her power seemed to feed off, to grow from, his. I don't love him: I don't like him: I'm afraid of him. She realised, though, she did want him, she was greedy for him. But here she was, sitting in this dull, exasperating room and he lay sleeping in the lounge below, and what was to happen never could, because the afternoon intended to go on for ever.

She flung her brush away from her and moved restlessly to the window. The dog, curled by the radiator, stirred. The sun was gone. The landscape climbed in bleak ledges, grey snow becoming grey sky with no discernible difference. There was an as yet faint, cold whistle seeping through the panes, a sound that would grow into the roar of night.

She didn't fear the alien scene before her. She knew what lay hidden—every rip, every vein, every pore of the moor. Here her father, with very little persuasion from his infant daughter, had climbed stunted hawthorns to peer and leer and laugh at her from out of sweet-scented branches. He had no dignity that man, she thought, and smiled to herself. Big, jovial, rude, crude, without any sense, without *her* sense, of what was 'proper'. She laughed. How she had loved him. He was with her yet. She first knew the moor through him and then through her own perception, a place where you could walk and the horizons remained distant. She thought of the man sleeping below, the man who said he came from the south. Could she, if necessary, use the moor as a weapon against him?

She was stilled by the notion. The moor, she knew, claimed victims, as any important soil should. Her thoughts came to a muddled halt. She must be rational. There was nothing more blinding than a mish-mash of half-apprehended intuitions. Things would happen or they wouldn't and she would meet them how she might.

Her sense of foreboding had returned. Broodingly she looked down at the barn and wondered what had happened there in the night. Her sense of isolation grew. Reality was linked with time going forward, but here it had evaporated. The sight, sense, taste, sound, the feeling of this afternoon, the essence of snow greyness, snow coldness, was forever.

She began to wander about, her feet measuring the limits of her prison. Jesus, if only she could get out. She stopped by the window and speculatively eyed the barn. If it were empty and safe surely her myriad fears would at last go away. Surely there must be unexceptional explanations for the abandoned farmhouse. Then she could enjoy herself with that man. No, no, she couldn't. What about her husband? Nevertheless she stopped more often by the window and stood gazing across at the barn. She made up her mind. She would investigate it.

Putting on her sheepskin jacket, she quietly opened the bedroom door. The dog cocked an ear, but his eyes were firmly closed. Softly she descended the stairs and crept across the hall to the lounge.

Leo was still deeply asleep, huddled, she thought, a man cowering from the elements. But here the elements were the soft warmth of Dermott's room, the gleam of parquet, the throb of brass, the secretive shadows of patterned objects. She found herself moving slowly round him, revelling in the power she had over this vulnerable, sleeping man. Why, I could stick him with a bread-knife in no time, she thought and laughed silently to herself. Her feet, her body, floated in some ancient, rhythmic dance; she was a priestess creating a time-old ceremony.

She left the room suddenly. Absurd! What did she think she was doing? Who did she think she was? The answer came back abruptly, devastatingly: 'My father's daughter.'

On the steps of the farmhouse she paused, breathing deeply. Cold, she thought. Like sucking an icicle. And in a moment of exhilaration she embraced the afternoon with its sky like a great cream-ware plate.

The boots she had borrowed were too large and her injured ankle banged painfully in one of them. She moved quietly through the snow she had cut earlier and then into his diggings. His work was not as neat and straight as hers, and some of the snow had fallen back in. 'Tha reads a man by 'is labour,' her grandmother had told her. But what did she read into this hastily dug passageway? The barn loomed up. She stopped, uncertain now. Snow which had got into her boots began to melt. Her feet were becoming numb.

The barn doors almost reached the roof of the stone structure, but almost at once she saw that a normal-sized door was cut into the left-hand side. She shivered, half-looking over her shoulder. The branches of the shattered tree by the farmhouse door began to shift. She sucked in her breath, moved forward and lifted the latch, worrying it. It wouldn't open. She put her shoulder to the door, but it didn't move. It was locked. Leo had locked it. Why would he do that? The wind slowly lifted her hair and let it settle again about her frozen face.

Could it be that the door was on the latch when he shut it, so that the lock automatically sprang to? She saw that the building had a small window, but she would have to dig her way through to it. Ought she to go back and try and find the key? Leo would have it, she thought intuitively. Leo was the key to everything.

Slowly she turned and made her way to the house. The green front door, still slightly ajar, seemed so familiar to her that bumps and cracks in its surface were like contours on her own body. The place is too familiar, she thought with a shiver. She realised suddenly that she didn't know it from the past, like her childhood homes. From the future, she thought. It's as though this place has always been waiting for me. The idea electrified her. What am I saying? What am I on about? It's not possible. And yet she had a momentary sensation of seeing her life from a distance, of seeing and discerning its pattern. Like love, she thought: that moment in love when you are no longer in your own skin.

She entered the house and firmly shut the door behind her. A place couldn't select a person: a person selected a place. But she was still uneasy. Perhaps there are times when you brush against something beyond reality and there's no making sense ot it. Why make a song and dance about it? Just accept it. That was how her father had dealt with it, she remembered, when he had held up a dock leaf to the rays of the sun and didn't see the leaf or the sun but some bouncing vision of life beyond. He had just accepted it. 'Some people have holes in their heads,' he had told her once; 'and they drop through them and experience things other people don't. They're not mad. It's as though they aren't sewn tightly enough into the fabric of their own time and sometimes fall out of it. Don't worry. Don't worry, little chicken. Enjoy it. Enjoy it all. By God, it's all you've got. All you'll ever have.'

She had thought he loved her: she had been quite sure in his love. But had it been an illusion? She had never

77

seen him since the day he had gone off with his lady love. She had waited and watched out for him, had even searched the streets of the town for him. But he was gone.

'Enjoy it,' he had told her. 'Enjoy it all ...' But she had never done that, she thought. She'd never enjoyed things to the full, never given life its due. She had been too afraid, too afraid of the arbitrary wrath of the gods. She knew now, though, that if this place ever released her she would take her courage in both hands, she would open herself up wide again and receive life, receive it all and trust that in doing so she wouldn't be destroyed.

Leo was still asleep. When she saw him she felt a treacherous ache. See how the corduroy cannot disguise those strong thighs, she thought. Her hand stretched towards him in sudden glee. She retracted it, trying to bury her desire, but it was more than his physical presence that invaded her. There was some secret recognition of each other, feelings which slid out from under consciousness and dwelled each within each. But I don't like him. I don't even know him. What's his second name? What's the colour of his eyes? She couldn't answer.

Clara, his first wife, the one he said had killed herself: he had loved her. There was love when he spoke of her. So he was capable of love, wasn't he?

Leo stirred in his sleep. She shook herself. She had come for the key, the key to the barn door: she wanted to get into the barn. She stole across the room to his anorak, which was carelessly flung across a chair. Just as she was passing him his hand caught her arm. In her fright she sank to her knees. 'I thought you were asleep,' she breathed. She remained quite still, her heart banging hurtfully about in its cage.

'You turned the television off,' he didn't let her go; indeed his grip seemed to tighten. His eyes were only half-open.

'You were asleep,' she winced.

'What were you doing, creeping about?'

'Creeping? I didn't want to wake you. You're hurting me.'

He released her, but she didn't yet dare move away.

He caressed her arm. 'Sorry. I suddenly thought—'

'What?'

'Moving so quiet. Gliding. So fragile. I thought "Clara" and I wanted to hang on.'

'You said she was dead.'

'Yes.'

'I need a drink.' She scrambled up.

'You've been out?' His voice was harsh.

'To see if it was thawing—getting warmer. It isn't. Oh dear, let me think. There're bottles in the kitchen. Wine. Sherry, too. Gin. You must have noticed.'

'My father's tipple, gin.' He stretched his limbs, luxuriating in the warm air. 'Oh, that's better. I needed that. I needed some sleep. He used to be a service man. In the army. Everyone still calls him Major, but I suspect he wasn't.'

'Why?'

He grinned. 'He never talks much about service life and you know what these old army types are usually like.'

'No.' If anyone she knew had been in the army they kept quiet about it. Pale, thin northern men to whom life outside the smoky regions was unreal.

'There you go. It's difficult to hold even an ordinary conversation with you. You don't lubricate—yes, that's the word, or is it "facilitate"?—ordinary conversation. You're bloody awkward. Well, most army men who retain their title years after they've ceased to serve are usually all tanks-and-the-Western-Desert sort of rubbish. Not my old man.' He was cheerful, expansive, benign almost. She kept a wary eye on him as she took off her jacket. 'Of course, he's the right image—military bearing, moustache, strangulated voice. He likes the word "one" as well. He's an expert in its use. Puts down

79

half the population with it, the old bastard.'

'You don't like him?'

'Of course I do. I admire him. What a front, what a cheek. He runs a driving school, and how they all jump to his command.'

'It must be an effort, if he's pretending to be something he's not. I'd find it an effort.'

'Everyone pretends to be what he's not,' Leo said shortly. 'We hint, we lie, we dress up to project a bigger, better, best "I". Besides, he enjoys himself, my old man. He enjoys being a Major. And whether he was or wasn't when he was in the services, he certainly is now.'

'Well, you could easily find out.' She was irritated. It wouldn't have taken her more than a day to discover the truth. 'Why don't you ask your mother? Ask *her*. Ask someone.'

He smiled. 'I haven't the passion you have for knowing all. The truth is usually so boring and has nothing whatever to do with reality. Besides, though my mother wouldn't lie, she would circumnavigate the truth in a totally confusing way. She could never say "yes" or "no" to anything. She fragments herself over any question and obliterates it. Did you mention drinks? I'll have a gin. I feel human again. It's amazing what sleep can do. I feel re-charged.'

'For what?' Her question was meant to be flippant, but it crackled anxiously.

He stared at her intently and then laughed. 'For anything that may come along.'

'It's going to be a cold night,' she muttered, hurrying out of the room, leaving him basking in the warmth of his sudden well being.

The kitchen was warm and quiet. Light, reflecting off the panes, moved sullenly through it. She could have been underwater, so silently silky did the atmosphere feel. Reality, her reality, seemed to be seeping from her. She wasn't convinced now that nothing was hidden in the drifting shadows. If she lunged forward with her fingers they might touch something, mightn't they?

She stared at the fish-slice, noting the gap in the rack of knives on the wall. There was a slight noise behind her, and she spun, almost lurching out of her frame. The dog looked at her, its patient amber eyes gleaming distantly through the end of the afternoon.

'I suppose you're hungry, aren't you?' she said and began to put a bowl of scraps together. 'I don't even know your name. I'll have to ask him that, won't I?'

She was still thinking of him, hearing his cheerful voice. He had looked younger, stronger, surer. Again she had an intuition of desolation, of tragedy imprinted on the bones of the old house, of its imprint on him, too. The rising wind suddenly rattled a pane, and she looked out at the snow, which was smoked through with the coming of night.

She began to get a tray of drinks together. If only something would happen, she thought. If only I knew one way or the other. All this waiting! For what?

She picked up the tray and walked towards the door. Suddenly she stopped, rooted in the quiet gloom, her nerve was gone. She could move neither back nor forwards. Her clinging hands froze on the tray. Her mind was petrified.

Slowly she built herself up into the terrifying vacuum. She would have courage, she wouldn't scream, she wouldn't cry, she wouldn't hide: she would have courage. If something happened in the long, coming night she would face it.

Her frozen hands began to shake, and she put the tray down. She opened the sherry she had included for herself, drank it from the bottle, in great spluttering gulps, and corked it up again before carrying the tray into the lounge. Never had she wanted David so much before, but he wasn't here, only his ghostly face, his slightly anxious eyes. And then she felt a sense of triumph, of relief too.

81

She wouldn't go to pieces after all. She was still all right, still had a fighting chance.

Leo was by the window, staring out across the snow. She said: 'I've fed your dog. What's his name, by the way?'

'Snubs. My second wife named him. She has a sentimental nature.'

She put the tray down. 'Second wife ...' The words rang in her head like an alarm bell. Why didn't he call her familiarly, by her name? Why didn't he call her Jane? 'So he's really her dog?' She poured out the drinks.

'That's right.'

'But he was out with you?'

'Yes.'

She took her sherry and moved to the fireplace, and he watched her, smiling a little. Opaque light from the window struck his glasses, so that he looked eyeless. She turned her back on him, but the menace behind bore on her with the weight of an avalanche. Again she fought against the disintegration of going on her bended knees and begging him ... begging him what? And she saw that there would be no one turning point in her battle against fear.

He said: 'I wouldn't call a dog Snubs. I'd give it a proper name. Animals have their dignity.'

'Yes.'

'She's a needlewoman. Embroidery. She teaches embroidery at the art school. Not a real artist.' There was scorn in his voice.

'Oh.'

'Sentimental. Fluffs her line. A—'

'What?'

'Never mind.'

'When did you meet her?' She had been sipping her sherry and she felt warmer now, surer, and she turned towards him. He was watching her.

'About eighteen months ago. On holiday. She told me

of the job going here. I suppose you could say I got it through her. She told Dermott about me.'

'You can't have been married long.'

'No.'

'Why is she lame?'

'A car crash. When she was a kid. She—'

'What?'

'Beautiful hair,' he murmured. 'That's what first attracted me, long, thick and glowing. Fine hands. Very finicky about her hands and nails. You're ... quite pretty.' His voice was soft. He was perfectly at his ease, and yet beyond his pleasantness she sensed there was something ... monstrous.

'There's nothing wrong with me,' she said sharply. 'I'm not lame or anything. But I'm not much to look at, not even pretty.'

'Ah. That's where you're wrong,' and he was laughing, 'though you camouflage yourself so well. All that hair. You sink so far into yourself, detach yourself so completely from your surroundings. I can't even guess what you're thinking. I ... love your secretiveness, your slyness. I think: Are you the Devil, or am I? For you're so hidden, Christie, you could be anything. Do you believe in evil?'

'No.'

He picked up his gin. 'Why on earth not?'

'Too pure. Too pure a concept. Good will go into the making of evil as bad will go into the making of good.'

'My God, what a cynic you are! How unlike Jane. No sentimentality in you. What an austere and comfortless place to be.'

'What?'

He grinned. 'In your mind.'

'One makes the best of it,' she said laconically. 'Do you? Do you believe in evil?'

He was silent. She could hear the tick of the clock in the hall. She had an extraordinary feeling of suspended animation, of being part of a dream.

83

Eventually he said coldly: 'It has its own ritual. Like good. The Devil has his own ritual.'

'What?' she asked.

'... ritual. Pattern. To make it bearable, I suppose. To make it all bearable.'

'What are you talking about?' She found she was shouting.

He showed even, gleaming teeth. 'You are frightened of me.'

'It'll make no difference.'

'What?'

'To—to ... it all. What I feel ... if I'm frightened ... it'll make no difference.'

'I don't follow. I don't understand. We always talk at cross-purposes. What are you trying to tell me?'

They stared across the room at each other, the eddies of darkness sliding between them.

'You are as evasive as my mother,' he said. 'What a pity.'

'Pity?'

'There'll be no time for preliminary sketches.'

'What do you want to sketch me for?'

'But I could never pin you down. Not on paper ...'

She saw that he was following some twist in his mind, some strand of thought that even if he spoke of it she probably could not follow its logic. Are his thought patterns normal, she wondered. But then, were hers?

He seemed to come to an end of his silent cogitations, for he announced: 'The snow will be gone soon. The weather will get warmer. It said so on the telly.'

'It did?' She felt a faint upsurge of hope, but even as she spoke the night was smudging the realities of the room. It grew in corners, climbed furniture, began to hang from the ceiling. 'There'll be a thaw?' She saw her husband in the brown lounge-diner of her home. He was sitting in the steel-and-leather armchair, his long legs propped up on the fireplace. The picture was complete in

84

her mind and radiating like a soap bubble. She felt weak at the knees. She sat down. Leo was still watching her speculatively. What was he planning? To distract him from whatever chain of thought he was now pursuing, she said: 'You've always lived in the south?'

'Bournemouth. I was brought up in Bournemouth. My mother and father settled there after the war. Suited my father's retired-major image. Money for cars in Bournemouth. His driving school prospered and they bought one of those Victorian houses which are all ceilings and draughts. It sounds a limited sort of existence and it was—very middle-class and proper, with piano lessons for me and thoughts of a career in the Church of England. I was religious in those days. Oh, I've told you that. Churches still do things to me ... the way sunlight sears through the dust and all the atoms shine like gold ...' He paused and stared moodily into his glass. 'Anyway, my father wasn't a limited man. It was only an impression he gave, an impression he made his living by: safe, secure, madam, you're all right behind the wheel with me. When I suddenly kicked the traces and got in at the Slade no one was more delighted than he. "No bullshit for you my boy!" My mother was alarmed. She thought of drugs and girls and dissipation, though she didn't say so. We had circumventory discussions about the arduous nature of an artist's work and how he needs all his strength for his vision, his pictures. So don't fornicate, don't take drugs and wear a woolly vest in winter.' He laughed, amused by the memory. 'You know, when I think of her I don't just remember her but I see the scraggy palm in our garden and the running red of fuchsia bushes. We had hedges of them to protect us from the prying eye of the tourist. I never see her out of her setting.'

'A sea-side town,' she murmured and wondered what it was like to be on holiday all the year round. Her long legs plunging into sand and the sagging, groaning rows of deck-chairs in front of her, beer bottles and orangeade buried to keep them cool. She heard and smelled the cold sea coming in, something hostile, not quite kept out by the knitting needles and tongues and babies' nappies screwed in plastic bags.

He smelled only the cotton print of his mother's freshly laundered dress and traced the gently fractured sentences of her speech, words that didn't make a point but lay on top of each other like slivers of skin, the last layer with a bloom that made all the others a proper supporting structure.

Christie, glancing at him, saw him differently now. His features were softened; his limbs flowed through the air like liquid from a jug. This was his core, she felt; but knowing this didn't put her at ease.

'It's different. Very different. All closed in,' he said.

'What?'

'Living in your town. When you have the sea at your front you are open-ended. But here the chimneys of the mills surround you like railings. And sometimes there isn't a wind at all. By the sea there's always a wind. It gives one a sense of being airborne, blown away! It's not the same here, not the same at all.'

'I wonder why you came, then.' Her voice was sharp, defensive. He was talking about her town.

'Because of Jane. I came because of Jane.'

'Your second wife?'

'Yes.'

He was closed in again now, morose. She shivered. The room was steadily getting colder. 'Can the heating have gone off?'

'What?'

'Perhaps the boiler's pilot has blown out. It's getting cold. Colder.'

'I shouldn't have left, you know,' he told her. 'This isn't my country. It's not ... how I am, how I live. This is savage!'

She thought of the streets in her town, air tangled with the taste of sulphur, dock leaves pushing up through concrete and the rumble-rattle of the Georgian windowed factories.

'Nowhere else seems quite real to me. Nowhere else seems hard enough, terrible enough. When I'm anywhere else … when I'm on holiday … I feel let off … playing truant from life … a bit guilty.' She stopped suddenly, feeling embarrassed because he was staring so intently at her. 'I'm sure it's gone colder. I'm sure the heating's turned itself off …'

'I … yes.' He, too, was embarrassed. He finished his drink. 'Christie.'

'Yes?'

'How old are you?'

'Twenty-four.' He is attracted to me, she thought. The knowledge flashed upon her, made her feel edgy, more unsure than ever. Her earlier desire for him was quite dead. She moved restlessly to the window. 'My God. Will it never thaw? Will it never end?'

'Oh yes.'

She spun round. There was something about him she couldn't yet quite grasp … some enormity of … and her confused thoughts broke down.

'I'll take a look at the boiler,' he said. He was grinning. He took his glass with him.

Alone in the room, she moved distraughtly about. The walls reached out, touched her. She veered into the hall and opened the front door.

She stayed quite still, breathing deeply. The white moor wasn't still. Its sifting and sighing had taken on a sharp edge. Plane after plane of snow grew perceptibly darker, and at the centre of it all was the dull yellow patch of sunset; it was scarred across with purple, a hurting bruise of star. She felt her spirit respond to this cold, alien world, which gave shape, beauty, even purpose to her own desolation.

Suddenly she chuckled, exulting in the hardness of the coming night, the hardness coming in her. After all, she needn't let herself be destroyed, she could be the destroyer. Her hands moved, exploding in the air and then remaining outstretched like a priest's.

She felt rather than heard him behind her. Slowly she turned. He was at the bottom of the hall, his eyes shining like a toad's from the inking well of darkness. Neither spoke, for there were only minor surface-things to say: the deep things were hidden in this cold and colder darkness. Carefully she closed the front door and went in again.

6

He was in the room at the head of the stairs. He had gone to bed quite early. He was still tired, he said; he hadn't slept much the night before. My God, how the house rattled. At times it seemed that the insistent noise came from inside her brain and not from outside at all. She kept walking to the bottom of the stairs and looking up at the closed door. Once she crept stealthily up and listened, but he made no noise, no noise at all. Twice she opened the front door, but the howling night drove her back: no way out. In the kitchen the dog slept; in the lounge the lights burned, as she twisted and turned and drove herself round and round the furniture, with mindless, frantic movements. He was so quiet. She had gone upstairs again. He was making no noise at all.

She was back in the lounge. She stood in the centre of the room, her hands on her ears. She wanted to scream: she needed her voice to go on and on for ever, never to stop. But later she was sure she hadn't made a sound, and now she was sitting down and very quiet. Her hands shook a little, but that was all. Earlier there had been tears on her cheeks, but not now. Anyway, what could she do? What could be done except wait until the snow melted?

She went upstairs again, this time to the bedroom she had made her own. The chimes of the grandfather clock floated up to her, telling her that it was too early to be so tired, but she was weary in a way she had never been before, as though her spirit were shutting out its lights one by one. She sat on the bed and surveyed the vast green field of counterpane, which seemed to float around her like clouds of summer grasses when the wind was warm and brisk—in the long, long scent-inhaled summers of the childish inner eye. Was she dozing already? Shouldn't she barricade the door against him? But in the early afternoon hadn't she desired him? It seemed lifetimes ago, so long that even the memory of the feeling was gone. Oh yes, she thought, the lights, my lights, are going out one by one and darkness is taking me. All the same she rose drunkenly to her feet and fought her way across the floor. She clutched hold of the chest of drawers and began to heave and pull. The chest lurched part-way across the door. Somewhere below, from the kitchen regions, the dog set up a nervous bark.

She gave up, weaving towards the bed and parting the covers. The open bed was one of the most beautiful sights she had ever seen: white sheets, sheets that covered England, would cover her—shivery, delicious, stinging sheets. And then she was still, curled in the centre of it all, warm now—received, she thought, with a sigh.

It came casually into her mind, the smell of wood smoke, of leaves burning in the autumn. She was creeping quietly along the boundary of wall and hedge, not because she was frightened of being seen, but because it delighted her. Stalking was a favourite method of locomotion. She paused at the gap in the hedge and saw Mr Beldon wielding his broom, savagely lifting the leaves to their fiery end. He was loudly singing a hymn because he was a Congregational man and scorned timid worship ... 'Rejoice to the heavens', and he did so lustily, blasting his soul upwards and outwards. Sometimes he and his wife took her mother to tombola in the church hall at the bottom of the estate. 'It's bingo really,' her mother confided, 'but it doesn't seem really respectable for a church.' If Mr Beldon was aware of the greeny eyes peering through the privet, he had the sense not to show it, and she sniffed and snooped, cocked an ear to his singing, and tasted the wood-smoke on the tip of her tongue, while her bottom, exposed to the slicing October wind, got bluer and bluer, and soon she was forced to dance away, whirring and twirling like the burning debris of summer.

She awoke, consciousness returning with a pop like gas jumping from an opened bottle. The smoke didn't belong to her past, her dreams; it was here and now, curling under the door of her barricaded bedroom. The house was on fire. She sat up, confused. She sniffed and tasted and blinked. She slithered off the bed and stuffed her arms into her jacket. Jesus, she thought, the house is really on fire. And then, as she pushed her feet into borrowed slippers: Shall I let him burn to death? But he hasn't done anything to me. He hasn't raised a finger against me. It's all in my mind.

Better safe than sorry? The jeering words danced in her head, soaring into an unholy jig. Better safe than sorry. The dog had set up a barking. She began to push the chest away from the door. A cylindrical pot, full of pencils, crashed to the floor. She put her shoulder against the chest and heaved it back into place. She opened the bedroom door. The smoke, curling along the landing, made her splutter. She snapped on the landing light.

He had his hand on the bannister, the smoke writhing through his nakedness. His small muscular body was like Pan's, and like Pan he danced on his toes as he turned to her. 'The smoke woke you up?' His head was tilted. He wore his glasses like armour.

'Yes.' She suddenly wondered whether he'd had the same thought as she, whether he had intended to leave her to the mercy of the fire. She winced and blinked in the smoke and asked 'Is it serious?'

'I was on my way. To look.'

She heard his bare feet pad down the stairs.

He shouted up: 'It appears to be coming from the

cellar!' His voice became distant. 'I'll take a look. You get some water lined up.'

She bundled herself downstairs and into the kitchen. The frenzied dog nearly knocked her over, and she grabbed him and thrust him into the dining-room. His demented body shook the door. She pushed her hair out of her eyes and stared about her. She filled two plastic buckets. Leo staggered through the kitchen door. 'That bag of rubbish in the cellar. Sugar paper. On fire.'

'Cigarette. Your cigarette. You were smoking down there.'

'Give me those buckets. Bring some water yourself.' The water slip-slopped behind him as he ran.

She filled the washing-up bowl, and as she went down he was coming back up the cellar steps with his empty buckets and they brushed by each other. The shock of touching him almost made her lose her footing. Jesus, she thought, as she swayed down the rest of the steps. He had switched on the cellar light, but she moved more as though by instinct to the source of the heat. As the fire devoured her water, she was momentarily hypnotised by its sizzling fury. She rushed back upstairs, careful to stand out of his way as he came through the kitchen door.

'We can control it,' he shouted. 'We can do it. As long as the floor boards above don't catch light, we can do it. You fling your water at those. Damp them down.'

She nodded and filled her bowl again, her smarting eyes dim with tears. At the top of the steps he took the bowl from her. She picked up his empty buckets. 'Could do with a hose,' she shouted.

'No. No hose. In barn. Used.'

She stumbled off with the buckets, while he disappeared into the choking smoke.

The fire died as quickly as it had flared up.

'Just got to the end of the rubbish,' he said. 'I kept the ceiling cool. Otherwise—'

'The whole house could have gone up?'

'Probably.'

They stood in the acrid cellar, he with a wet handkerchief over his mouth and nose, but otherwise naked, she with her eyes shut against the smoke. She became aware of his hand under her elbow, as he led her up the steps into the hall. Did he feel this shocking current which his touch generated in her? Did he feel anything at all? It's like being a girl again, she thought, a teenage girl.

'We'll shut the cellar door and open the front one,' he said. 'See if we can get rid of the smoke in the house.' The pressure on her arm was gone. 'Not a big fire. Just a small one. Nothing to worry about.'

'You're sure it's out?' She stumbled against the wall by the dining-room door.

'I'll keep an eye on things.'

'My eyes hurt. Horribly.'

'Bathe them. Bathe your face in water. Christ! I wish that damn dog would shut up.'

'He's frightened.' She had opened her eyes. She was fascinated by the sight of him, his shape, his size, his nakedness. She shivered violently. He retreated to the stairs, his streaked skin gleaming in the light. Fingers from one of her hands floated in the air, gliding across it like twigs on a pond. 'You've nothing on,' she whispered.

'No. Didn't think. Wasn't time. Sorry.'

'Would you have come for me?'

'What?'

'To tell me about the fire. Would you have got me out?'

'Got you out? It was only a little bit of a fire. Nothing to worry about. Nothing at all. Better get that door opened, get some air in. Better get something on. You make the tea. See to the dog. Christ, what a din.'

He turned and bounded to his tasks.

She didn't stir until his bedroom door was closed behind him. The vision of his moving body was sinking

93

through her. She jerked to as the cold air snaked through the front door. She let the dog out of the dining-room. It buried itself into her and she idly stroked it and teased out its ears and surrounded it with her warmth. She lifted an ear-flap to tell it some of her thoughts and it wriggled and buried its head deeper into her.

Why did she even think about Leo? She always, in the end, said no; she always denied herself pleasure. And it wasn't only men: she said no to practically everything, because it was the safe thing to do. She was a negative woman.

She put out the cups and bathed her face. The grandfather clock in the hall struck four. My God, she thought, nearly a new day. Perhaps today I shall get out. Perhaps today it will all end. She drew back the kitchen curtain. Here night whirred and banged and gave no hint that it would not go on for ever.

She was aware of him before she heard or saw him. She sensed his coming. Not love, she thought: something dark. Fear?

He wore a red silk Paisley patterned dressing gown which didn't fit. 'Dermott was a short man,' he said. 'A bit of an actor. A bit of an image maker.' He caressed the edge of the gown. 'I like the feel of silk. It feels like cigars, like a Rolls.' He laughed at himself.

Carefully she poured the tea. She was feeling light-headed. What if I pour this boiling pot all over him, she thought. He won't be fit for much after that!

'It's quite unfair that a bastard like that ... a real pig of a man ... Dermott ... should be so good.'

'Good?'

'It's really there ... that something which ... how can I? ... the board is there, the paint is there, like the rest of us ... but something is added, something transforms it all, makes it work. We all have vision, inner light, but *his* reflects up again in the paint. I'm not making any sense. I—'

'You're telling me you're no good. Not a good artist.' She savaged him.

He was silent, staring at her. His quiet drove through the room, through her head. Her mind began to move in frantic circles. She had upset him, hurt him. She had known how to belittle him. Wasn't that knowledge dangerous?

Suddenly he bellowed: 'Christie, you will get your neck wrung! Has anyone ever tried to wring your neck?' He thrust himself towards her, half angry, half playful.

She retreated. 'I don't know why I said that. I expect you're really very good.'

'You have to be big in an unexplainable sense to be good, really good. I'm just a small man.'

She was now so frightened she could hardly breathe. She knew she had torn him wide open, stuck her hand into some terrible wound. Though he spoke quietly, though he tried to be amused, she felt his power, his wildness, his misery. It was held in check only by a thread of self-mockery. 'I'm just a small man.'

His hand moved towards her, was raised against her though he was too far away to do her any harm. The bent finger nails seemed to push into her eyes. 'In some strange way I feel you know me so well.' His voice was matter-of-fact. 'You know all about me.'

'I don't,' she was shouting. 'No. No I don't. Not at all!'

'That's fear.' He was jeering at her. 'You are afraid of what you know. You won't admit it—the whole of it—to yourself.'

'What do I know?' she muttered.

He was waiting for her, she realised, waiting for her to make some move towards him, and she wanted to. But she wouldn't. She felt that her only chance of survival lay in her independence. In her own will.

'We can try to get through. They will surely have salted even the moor roads by now. It's not so far, not so far from this farmhouse to the road.'

He touched his chin, stroking it gently. 'I can't imagine it.'

'What?'

'Getting out of here—ever getting out of here. Can you?'

'Of course we'll get out,' she shouted. 'We'll get out tomorrow. We've only been stranded a day and two nights.'

'I seem always to have been in this place. Time means nothing here.'

She knew what he meant, because hadn't she found it so? It was as if The Bield were spinning through space and nothing existed beyond it. However, she said: 'We can't stay here forever. Dermott will come back, for one thing. Perhaps his companion as well. The meal was laid for two.'

Leo began to laugh. He laughed so much that he had to lean his body against the kitchen units. He laughed and laughed until he was in an agony of laughter.

She observed his mirth and felt impelled to smile. Her smile became broader and broader until it changed to a tentative giggle. At what? The dog pranced on its front paws and uttered an occasional, companionable bark. Even the knives hanging on the wall danced to his bodily pleasure.

She stopped laughing first, and her hand reached out and grasped at an aspirin bottle which had been left on the kitchen window sill. She hadn't got a headache, nor even the beginnings of a cold, but she was aware of agony, whether hers or his she couldn't say. It needed alleviating now, before it became more unbearable.

She took two pills. As he became more solemn, she said: 'What's so funny? I don't see what's so funny. Oh, I'm going to bed. It's too early to do anything now, but tomorrow we'll get out of this place.'

'Christie.'

'What?'

'We'll never do it. We'll never get out of here. Don't you know that?'

'Oh, yes we will. We'll get out,' she said steadily. 'Don't worry about it.'

'Christie.'

'What?'

'Why did you marry your husband? What's his name?'

'David. I sometimes think I did it because I wanted to be like everyone else, that there was no other reason. All my friends were getting married. I needed to be like everyone else, a proper kind of person. That's what I sometimes think.' She began to tremble. 'I must go to bed. I feel very tired now.'

'Christie.'

'What?'

'What do you do? What's your job?'

'I work in a library. That's me. A bookworm. A worm, all right. A person that hides away from everything, everyone. That's the essence of me. If you're a worm-like human you can't hide in holes, you can't bury yourself out of sight in the earth, so you hide by being like everyone else, by being indistinguishable from everyone else.'

'But why must you hide?'

'The gods may see me and envy me and bring wrath about my head. I think I'm frightened of being happy, whole, in case I get found out and am destroyed. So I hide away—to be safe, you know. So I'll feel more safe.'

He was suddenly smiling. 'But I found you out, didn't I? Hiding in the wardrobe. You can't hide away from me, Christie love.'

She considered. 'No. I don't think I can.' It was as if they were in possession of secret access to each other, some subterranean channel of communication. But what they silently told each other she didn't know.

'You tell me this—about being worm-like—and I

believe you. But it's very strange ... I feel you could be—you have it in you—what? Terrible. A terrible woman.'

'Well, well ...' and she grinned. 'I may be a mouse but I will be a lion.'

He was staring at her again. He kept staring as if by looking at her he would find the solution to some problem confronting him. Suddenly he turned away: 'All right. Go to bed. You might as well get some sleep.'

When she went upstairs the dog followed her, its nose at her heels. It rarely, if ever, sought out Leo as a companion, she realised. But, of course, it had been his wife's dog. Then why had it been with Leo on the night he was stranded? She looked back down the stairs. She saw only splinters of light cast by lit rooms. The front door was still open, and the hall moved and cracked and grunted as it strained against the forces of the night. 'Terrible. A terrible woman.' Was he trying to find companionship for his own monstrousness? But he wasn't a monster, was he? Her head began to whirr. She ought to go back and close the front door, but she was too tired. Let the night come in, let it pick the house clean.

She shut herself and the dog in her bedroom. It went unbidden to its favourite place by the now cold radiator. She struggled out of the jacket and let it fall to the floor. She ought to move the chest back against the door. Was she afraid for her wifely virtue, or her life? She left the door unprotected and climbed into bed. She was quite sure Leo hadn't yet made up his mind about her. After all, had she made up her mind about him?

But what kind of ground could ever be found between fear and need? 'It's not as though I love him, or even like him,' she told herself again. 'He excites me, though. I want him.' But wasn't that something, wasn't that a start? It seemed years since she had hungered for anyone quite like this, in this unthought, greedy way. 'I'm being stupid,' she drowsily told the dog. 'There's too much of my father in me ...' Her limbs shuddered and curled closer.

She didn't hear the door being opened half-an-hour later, she didn't even stir when Leo bent down to examine her. His regard was thorough and detached. He observed every curve, every shadow of her, noting how her substance patterned her surroundings. The dog opened an eye and closed it again. He stole out and stayed outside her door for a few moments, listening to her sleep. He smiled to himself. He began to hum as he moved fleet-footed back across the landing.

She knew when she awoke that it was late. Motes of sunlight climbed down from the window pane. A dog's eye, caught in a shaft, gleamed beadily. 'I expect you want feeding again,' she grumbled sleepily. The dog made a soft whine and she heard a bumping which must be its tail.

Another noise—a great slurping, slithering noise—came from over her head. A chunk of grey momentarily filled the window and then crashed and splashed below. She blinked in the returned sun. The thaw, she thought. My God, it's happening. I can go home after all.

She swung off the bed, this time mindful of her sore ankle, and guided herself gingerly to the window. She wove in and out of light as thin and metallic as a needle; and Leo, who had silently come to the door, thought of her as part of a Burne-Jones tapestry.

'I've brought you some tea,' he said. She turned round, her face as pale as wax and her eyes blue, green, brown—he couldn't say, for the darkness changed, forever different, like midnight water. 'Time you were up,' he said. 'I thought it time you were up. I've brought you some tea. To wake you gently. You still look tired.' He felt dazed by her, by the brown glitter of her hair, by the drooping of her breasts, the spread of a half-turned thigh. He told himself he couldn't desire her, there was nothing left in him to desire with; but tenderness grew. It was through this very tenderness that he got his first intimations of terror.

'The cup,' she said sharply. 'You're going to drop it.'

'I—'

'Are you all right?'

'What?'

'The cup!'

He put it down on the chest of drawers. 'I'm ill. Perhaps flu is coming on ... or something. I suddenly felt—quite awful.' His hair, a frizzy shock about his face, seemed to emphasise his momentary loss of control. Its wiry voltage trembled in the light. Had he lost his nerve? She felt quite cold, but he assured her: 'I'm all right now. Don't know what it was.'

'Someone walk over your grave?' Her voice crackled. 'But it was nice of you. The tea. Nice of you to think of it.'

His voice had returned to normal. 'The smoke has gone. It's a bit of a mess down in the cellar.'

'Dermott will be displeased, won't he?' She thought of the night, of the choking, stumbling chaos, of his nakedness, the smoke licking the muscular body as he danced on his toes like Pan. The image began to work hotly in her mind, its lava spilling over, destroying some of her caution. Could it be I don't love David? What is love? The feeling I had for my father? She turned abruptly from the window. And what about Leo? He seemed, this alien man, to invade her, colouring her thought, enriching, expanding, making her more powerful. Why should this be so, when where Leo walked so surely walked too ... annihilation?

'Are you cold?'

'Cold?'

'You're shivering. It's still very cold. I've turned the heating on, of course, but it will take a while for these old stones to warm up.' He retrieved the tea cup. 'Come on. Have it—'

She took it from him. She didn't, couldn't, look at him.

She retreated to the window, staring sightlessly out. He moved up to stand beside her. Their bodies weren't touching, but each was as violently engrossed in the other as if they were making love.

This time it was Leo who moved away. 'It's thawing,' he said. 'It's the start of the thaw.'

'We can go home soon.'

'Home?' he asked sharply.

'It doesn't seem real any more. Home,' she whispered. 'Nothing beyond here seems real. It's all here. Being here.'

'You live in the town?'

'In an open-planned semi-detached. Open-planned estate.'

'Don't you like it?'

'It's—featureless.' She smiled suddenly. 'Like semolina pudding.'

Uneasily they both listened to the slithering, slurping snow over their heads.

'No. It's not forever.' He was frightened. 'It's an illusion, after all. It has seemed so permanent. What did you say? It's all here. Being here.'

Snow crashed into the farmyard. There was a steady dripping noise.

'The Volkswagen.'

'What?'

'I crashed the car. It went off the road into a ditch.'

'Yes.'

'Well, I said, didn't I? I must have said. Christ—'

'What?'

'What's that?'

He came to stand beside her again. They stared across the snowy farmyard.

'There! To the right of the tree. No, there. It's a—man. His—'

'Coat. A coat!'

'Isn't that ... There. Hand—'

'No!'

They stared together at the rising lump of soft greyness exposed by the warming winds.

She moved from him fractionally. 'A man.' Snow sluiced down the window. She was aware of the distant sound of running water. By nightfall the whole mountain would be awash. By nightfall most of the snow would be gone.

'He doesn't seem to have a head,' she said. 'Can you see a head, Leo?'

7

They were at the door of the farmhouse. The clouds were rent open, the mountains exposed to the winter sun: all gleamed with a cold, metallic brightness. The fierce shadows the buildings threw were impenetrable. The object they had seen from the bedroom window lay on the far side of the yard, near the window of the barn—almost, she thought, as if it had been tossed out. But a body couldn't be pitched through such a small window, could it? So softly vulnerable, so pathetic. A corpse on the hygiene of an endless hospital sheet. 'Oh God.' This time something *was* there. It wasn't her imagination. That gruesome, abandoned thing was real. 'Dermott?' she whispered.

'It's his coat.' The voice was cold. 'Leather. He liked to wear leather. It was one of his things.'

'I can't see a—his head.'

Leo was silent. He shuffled a little further back in the doorway to avoid the dripping lintel.

'Perhaps it's buried still. The snow's still thick. Very - thick. Perhaps the—his head—perhaps it's buried.'

He said nothing. She felt herself contract, diminishing the area of attack. The air was so clear, so sharp, and she was so concentrated that she felt she could penetrate through it into the denseness of mountain rock itself. 'I can see a hand.'

'Hand?'

'His hand.' She thought she oughtn't to let Leo move behind her so she too retreated into the hall. 'We shall have to dig out to him. It'll be hours before we can walk over. The snow's too deep.'

'I've made you some breakfast.' His voice was toneless. 'Eggs and bacon. It's in the warm store.'

'I can't eat!' She was outraged.

'If you—we—are going to dig, you'll need something hot in you.'

'I'd be sick! What's the matter with you? Don't you realise—'

'What?'

'A man out there and you—'

He was quiet again. She couldn't understand his awkwardness, his lack of urgency.

He said stubbornly: 'It's a coat.'

'A coat doesn't have a hand! Jesus Christ.' Tears rolled down her face, but she was more sorry for herself than for the obscene lump in the snow.

'You're a fool.' For the first time she was aware that he was angry, that his abrupt words were cover for an incomprehensible fury.

'I—'

'Digging!' he shouted. 'Digging in shadows!'

They were rigidly at attention in the confines of the shadowy hall. She daren't look at him, daren't even contemplate him. The clock beat out its seconds, remorseless, moving ever on. That is the secret of life, she thought—not my life, not his, or Dermott's, but life: it will go on. She had pushed her hands into her thighs, bracing her fingers so that they shouldn't tremble so. Her back was shielded by the wall.

His voice was soft. 'I'll start. I'll start the digging.' He had been thinking, thinking so deeply that he had completely withdrawn from her, and now his tone was hesitant as he re-established communication. 'You eat the breakfast I made and then you can take over for a bit.'

What else had he been considering? What had he been

planning? 'All right,' she said dully.

'Where did you put the spade?'

'In the long cupboard in the kitchen. By the fridge.'
You could split open a skull with a spade. Stove it in.
What did dead people look like? What did Dermott look
like? Better shut away in their coffins. Better not seen.
Death could be majestic if you didn't concern yourself
with the details. It could be music and rituals in church, it
could be sun pouring through stained-glass windows, it
could be knotting groups swaying by clinking damask
and boiled ham sandwiches and tea laced with rum.

He had got the spade in his hands and was by the
kitchen door. His shoulders were hunched, powerful, and
the fingers firmly squeezed the wooden handle. He was
almost indolently at ease, staring at her. She felt he was
watching for one chip, one crack in her calm, one
opening to slice into. An insidious, magical signal
between them could trigger her destruction. But she was
whole, impervious, as hard as marble. Steadily she met
his gaze. If I ever get through this, she was thinking, if
ever I live through this moment I'll sharpen up one of
those kitchen knives and keep it in my pocket. He won't
find me easy to kill. I won't let him easily dispose of me.
She was burnished with her cold anger, quiet, powerful
in the shadows, as potent in his head as out of it.

'Christie.'

'What?'

'You feel beautiful.'

They were silent, and then he said: 'Your breakfast.'

'What?'

'In the warm store—.'

The spade touched her as he walked by. He seemed to
thrust it to one side purposefully, so that she felt the steel
against her leg.

'You feel beautiful" he had said. He looked back at her.
He was by the open door. His hair was wildly caught up
in the sunlight, so that, like a Catherine wheel, it sent off

105

glittering sparks; and, like the centre of a Catherine wheel, his face was black.

She heard him chuckling. Was he mad? Had she been living with a madman? Well, it made no difference. Mad or sane, she would try to destroy him if he threatened her. As the front door shut, she was left in the gloom. She stayed very quiet and gathered to her the strength in the air, the house, the earth under her feet. She sucked its magic into her. I can be powerful, she thought, awed.

She went into the kitchen. The dog, appearing from nowhere, made her aware of its presence by rubbing her leg. She cut up some scraps and put them on a plate. 'There,' she said absently. 'There you are. What's your silly name? What was the name she gave you? That Leo's wife?'

She took her breakfast out of the warm store. Leo had taken pains with it: egg, bacon, fried bread, tomatoes appetisingly arranged. A labour of love? She sat down. She felt confused. She was attracted to him, too. But that would make no difference. Love and destruction. They weren't, she felt, incompatible with Leo. Had others burnt so that he might rise and live and know himself through their ashes? Well, it didn't matter, not really. Time might go on and on, but there was little left to them, even for speculation. Their world was flat, like a plate; it had no third dimension, and very soon they were going to fall off it.

But was this all true? What she was thinking? Was it real? Here she was now, eating the breakfast he had made for her because it might be the last meal she would eat for some time—the meal before combat. But why should I think so?

The feeling persisted. She had been very near death that morning, and she would be very near it again before the day was out. After this day she might never wake up and feel the morning. She didn't know what kind of tragedy had engulfed The Bield, but she had been sucked into it.

106

Was her part that of victim, unless by some fantastic act of will she could change the nature of things?

'Oh Christ!' she told the dog. 'Am I imagining it all?' But she hadn't imagined the body by the barn, had she? And suddenly she could eat no more of the breakfast Leo had cooked for her. The hand which reached out for the teacup was shaking. 'Is it real? Is it all real after all?' and she talked out loud, so she could hear her voice, run her tongue over her existence. She got up abruptly and went over to the knife rack. 'Nothing too big. Something that will easily fit into my pocket.' She was gazing at the gap in the rack marked by the fish-slice. Do I really believe I could kill him, she wondered. Shut out the light? Take away those fingers in the grass and the sumptuousness of hard stomach against hard earth ... Away. All away? For the second time since she had come to The Bield she chose a knife as weapon and set the electric sharpener to work. He couldn't fail to notice it was missing. He would realise she had it. Perhaps that was as well. It might warn him off. Her thigh against his ... she had felt it this morning as they stood by each other in the bedroom. She had forgotten what life was all about until she met Leo. She had forgotten to be alive.

Did loving someone make it easier to kill them? 'But Leo is aggressive! He's not going to be easy at all.' She slid the knife from the sharpener. She was fascinated by the burnished blade. 'It's quite beautiful. The way it shines. The way it's cold. Like the universe is cold. Like God is cold.' She began to feel dizzy with excitement or fear, she couldn't tell. Suddenly she realised she was euphoric. It was going to be all or nothing, all or nothing. She slipped the knife into her pocket. She'd never felt so alive, so good, so altogether. Her muscles rippled. She could no longer keep still. She twirled.

The dog watched her with patient, accepting eyes. What had it been witness to? For a moment it didn't seem ridiculous to ask it and get an answer. The laws of logic seemed suspended—superseded by those of magic. And yet here she was now, scraping off her breakfast into the scrap bucket and running the water so that she could wash up. She thought of Leo outside, shovelling through the snow ... 'digging into shadows.' His voice had been bitter. He hadn't wanted to involve her. But she felt impelled to find out what had happened at The Bield. And she thought of the body in the snow. Her hands floated up through the washing-up water like dead fish. Would she, she wondered, calmly go about some chore if an H-bomb were falling through the sky? She stared in bewilderment at the water, at her hands, at the snow beyond the window.

Well, what *did* you do if a body lay in your back yard? What were the conventions? You screamed, called the police, fainted perhaps? But for all these things you needed an audience, you needed people. It had nothing to do with The Bield. The Bield was cut off from the world, spinning in this capsule beyond reach, almost beyond thought. She and Leo ... she and Leo and the thing! Well, they would have to get by without patterns, without rituals. They'd have to find their own way of getting through.

Determinedly she wiped her hands on her trousers. Whatever you did in such a situation, you didn't wash up. Surely in those waters madness lay.

Resolutely she turned, faced the door and then marched out. Oh God, she thought bleakly, I wish I were home with my husband, with the neighbours. With Juliette's waters which broke in the market, and Maureen with her backache. I'm not capable of all this. I can't manage it. I can't rise to it! Nevertheless she opened the front door. Her heart was uncomfortable; her knees slid together for company. She shielded her eyes against the running sun. Leo was sending up showers of snow. He used his spade, his energy, in a careless, easy fashion, as though he had never heard of conservation, as though his power were limitless.

I would never wield a spade like that, she thought. Too many peasants in my ancestry, too much hoarding and starving and meanness in me. 'Shall I take over?' she shouted. Christ. We might be digging a vegetable patch.

He turned in the wavering trench he had created, his face flushed, his breathing clouding his head like an engine with steam up. 'All right.' His voice was cool enough and there was something else in it, in him. Laughter? She was shocked. She purposefully advanced along the trench towards him. There was this business of getting the spade off him. Her hand was in her pocket and she had hold of the handle of the knife. Her hair was teased up, and it lashed about her head in the steady wash of wind. 'How ferocious. You look like Medusa. Those black-brown snakes of yours writhing like mad.' Yes, he is laughing at me, she thought. But where is the joke? How can Dermott's body be funny?

'There's a dead man. There's a dead man, there—' she said tightly.

'So you say. So you say, Christie—' he jeered gently.

She looked across a bank of snow which was illuminated by the watery light of its own destruction. The black leather was carelessly heaped. A collar flapped. But no head.

Her hair stood on end. 'There's a body there!' she screamed.

She was distraught, but not distraught enough for her hand to relax on the knife which nestled in her pocket. It was as though there were two people in her: a terrified, frantic being, and a cold, calculating watcher who stared through the violent disturbances.

Like the eye of the storm, he thought, and darkness touched him, reminding him of his mortality.

He gave her the spade. 'You're getting hysterical,' he said brusquely.

It was her turn to laugh—but her laughter was

short-lived, killed by her central coldness.

He reached out to her. 'Christie.'

She moved back. 'I don't know. I don't know about all this. I don't know about death. What does one do? It's obscene.'

'It's not a body!'

'How do you know?'

'It doesn't look like a body, does it?'

'What?'

'There's no head. There's no bloody head!'

'You are trying to say ... it's not real?'

'I don't know.' He was mumbling. 'I don't know what I mean.'

'Do we have to do this? Do we have to do all this?' She was holding the spade with two hands, its blade turned towards him.

'What do you mean?'

'Can't you tell me about it?'

'Tell you what?' He was shouting. His hands moved up defensively, like a boxer's.

She backed away down the trench, backed away from her question, from his possible answer. They remained silent, staring at each other. He wanted to gather her in, she wanted to creep to him, but they remained separate. She felt she wouldn't survive if she didn't defend her boundaries, didn't keep him out.

'Damn this wind.' He shook snow out of his hair. 'Well, you'd better get on with the digging, I suppose. Have you fed the dog?'

'Yes.'

'I suppose it will have to be coffee. Too early for whisky.' He was already ambling back down the trench to the farmhouse.

She began her digging, using the spade neatly, economically. She looked up occasionally to check her direction and then her eye momentarily sang with snow and the blurred image of leather.

110

'None of it's true. None of it's real. None of it's true,' she told herself over and over again, as if she were saying a childhood prayer. Amen, amen, amen. But she enjoyed the digging. Her body was warm and she used it well. She realised that excellence was a pleasure.

The nearer she got to the hump in the snow, the more her personality seemed to diffuse. It ran through her warm body into past summers, into the light of single poppies in fields, into reedy waters which gibbered in random sun.

He moved quietly through his zig-zagging trench, through her straight work. He said: 'I'll take over now.'

She stared at him, bemused. Was he real, was the object in the snow real? She was so far in herself that she felt that if she closed her eyes she could drift away in the sounds and scents of her being and never come back. She kept her eyes open. 'My ankle's aching again,' she said. 'I must have rubbed it on the boot.'

'How did you hurt it?'

'You *know*. I said. I must have done. The Volkswagen—when it crashed. The car seemed to turn upside down.' Her whole world had turned upside down, hadn't it?

He got hold of the spade. 'Christie.'

'What?'

But he couldn't say he loved her, for surely that wasn't true. He hadn't known her for more than a day. Was it that he pitied her? Horror spilt in his mind like a black stain. He mustn't let her really reach him, touch him. He had known since the middle of the night how it must all end, hadn't he? And he wished to make it beautiful. He wished for a masterpiece. That called for detachment. 'Christie.'

'What?'

'It's a coat. It's a discarded coat. Dermott's coat. Look properly.' He began to smile at her, at the coat. Then he cackled. 'Christie, you idiot!' Now he was laughing, using the spade as a crutch for his shaking mirth.

Christie studied the object and saw he was right. The snow had filled out the coat and twisted it into its grotesque shape. Beyond it lay a glove, fingers stuck up. Beyond that again was light blindingly reflected from the barn window, so that the whole was haloed, like a religious picture. 'Well, a coat.' she said dully.

'A coat!' he cackled.

'It looked like a body. It really did look like a body.' She didn't feel relieved. If Dermott's body wasn't there, where was it? 'You knew all along, didn't you?'

'Knew what,' he spluttered.

'That Dermott wasn't there? Dermott's body?'

'Corpse? Don't you mean headless corpse?' The spade wobbled with a fresh burst of his laughter. 'If you could have seen your face. A coat! Just Dermott's coat. That's all. That's all, Christie.'

'Leo.' she shouted.

'What?'

'You—'

'What do you want to know?' he taunted. 'What do you want to ask? Go on. Ask me.'

'I— Did ...' But what did she want to say? She felt panic-stricken. Too near the precipice.

'A headless corpse. A headless corpse indeed!' Leo was still chuckling. 'Who did you think had lopped off Dermott's head? Me?' He reached out and took her arm. His head was thrust down towards hers. Light cracked off his glasses. 'Think of the problems. Think of the problems, m'dear. Did he lie down and stretch out his neck to make it easy? I can't even chop wood!' He was laughing again. She tried to pull herself free, but his grip was tight. 'Well, well. What do you think? What do you think I did?' He could hardly contain his glee.

She stared up at him through narrowed eyes. There was something ... just below the surface ... something sliding about behind his skin ... it was obscene. She remembered tales of princes turning into frogs. But was

112

this prince really a frog? Suddenly she was laughing, her mirth skittering along the borders of hysteria, and he was laughing, too, and now they clung to each other, swaying and roaring.

From beneath his glasses two tears emerged. 'You thought it was a corpse.'

'I really did.'

'D-Dermott's body!'

'Yes!'

'Y-you thought I'd chopped his head off!' Their laughter echoed on the skeletal drum of farm buildings.

'W-wh—'

'What?'

'L-Leo—'

'Yes?'

'Where is it? He? I mean Dermott?'

'I-I s-sliced him up. Minced him. Spaghetti bolognese!'

Fresh laughter engulfed them. The collar of the coat, which had been flapping like a flag, dipped. The fingers of the glove slowly collapsed. Water ran out of the seams.

'L-Leo—'

'Hush. Hush. Hush m' dear,' He was kissing her. He thought tenderly: 'It will have to be a masterpiece. Nothing less for her.' Well, it was a pity. A shame. But there would be other women. There were always other women. Would he even remember her face in a month's time? Or would it be like the recollection of a perfect summer's day, a distant, glowing bubble in the mind? His fingers, in the silk of her hair, trembled in delight.

He wasn't sure when he let her go, but she was drifting from him, moving ever further from his reach. 'Leo.'

'What?'

'I never really thought—'

'What?'

'That you killed him.'

'Oh, but you did, Christie. You do.' He pushed back his frizzing, haloing hair. He said gently: 'You thought I'd chopped off his bleeding head.'

'You—'

'No, no. You don't trust me an inch. Oh you don't, love. You think me mad, a madman with an axe. Chop, chop. Off with his head. Their heads!'

'Yes!' It was a wail, a cry for help.

But though he regarded her lovingly he made no move, no effort to still her fears. Building slowly in him was an excitement he knew would some time that day reach ecstasy. There was plenty of time. He liked there to be plenty of time, so that his soul could expand with that curious sense of wellbeing which came from power, perfect power ... Godhead. Yes, there was still plenty of time. He ought to have a record—some remembrance of her. Faces haunted him only in absence. Oh, the joy of it all. He was expanding minute by minute, filling the dank windy voids of universe. I am God. God is me.

Numbly she moved back down the diggings to the farmhouse. The dog, sitting primly inside the front door, greeted her. She looked back at Leo. Is he mad, she wondered. The way he ... what? stared at her? But she didn't think him mad. Couldn't a man commit an insane act by choice? A will to be evil? She shuddered. But it hadn't been Dermott's body, had it? How he had laughed at her. He had known, hadn't he? He had known Dermott wasn't lying in the snow. She thought of the coat, of the glove, of the way the sun blindingly came off the window of the barn. The images shimmered in her mind. If she had dug a little more she would have got to the barn window. She could have looked in and ... what, what? She seemed possessed by the thought of evil, something hidden, something just about to be found. She was standing in the hall by the stairs now. Her body was sliced through by a knife of light from the front door.

'Well, what are you going to do now?' He had propped the spade by the hall door. 'How else shall we amuse ourselves this merry morning? How else shall we

114

pass the time until the snow melts?'

'I'm going to do the things I haven't done. Get washed. Dressed properly.'

'Start the morning again?'

'Yes.'

'And hope it will turn out differently?' He snorted with laughter.

'What will you do?'

'Prepare myself.'

Her heart bumped. 'What?'

'For leaving, of course. For leaving this place. We'll be able to go before dusk. The snow's melting quickly now.'

'Yes, yes. It's—' She let out her breath in jagged relief. 'Oh my God.'

'What?'

'What will it be like? Going home again.'

'Home. Really going home?' He was mocking her.

'Yes.'

'Yes,' he agreed softly. 'You will be going home, love.'

She turned and hurried away from him, up the stairs to her bedroom.

She performed her toilet meticulously. She tidied the bedroom. I might be a guest getting ready to leave an hotel, she thought bewilderedly as she turned back the bed. But it was the small things that bound her into life, into reality. What was real about the leather coat, which was going down like a punctured football, or a subsiding glove? What was real about the uneaten meal, the bloodstain on the dining-room floor? She saw them, she experienced them, but she didn't relate them to anything. She was reminded of the people with her on the holiday beach, the chattering and clicking of knitting needles, the squeals of children, and beyond, filling the horizon, the implacable sea moving coldly up the shore. How did one put the two halves of the picture together? How did life and death become whole? She was shivering again. She must somehow turn her mind off, divert it.

She must try and conjure up blanket-warm images.

I don't fit in, she thought distressed. I'm not like them, like the other women on the estate. It was as though I was marked out to carry some burden of terrifying knowledge. I'm just playing the part of wife. There's so much of me unused by the role ...

She wandered over to the window. She stared at their diggings. The landscape was racked apart, darkness oozing from the wounds. She turned her back on it. The familiar room, with its objects now in some disarray, comforted her. It was all so reasonable—the bed, the chest of drawers, the functional pots for pencils and ash. She had so much difficulty in getting to know life. It seemed to move away from her so quickly, in smoking Novembers, in aching heavy Julys. She had never been able to grab it all to her. Like scent. The incredible scent of bluebells drifted into her head and was gone. She couldn't retain it.

She felt that if she put all this confusion of thought into words only Leo, of all the people she knew, would be able to understand her and in understanding would help her to bring order to the primaeval growths which choked her mind.

But though Leo could help her, she knew he wouldn't. He was following his own obsessions. Out there, out in the snow, he had looked at her as though she weren't a person at all but a tool, a piece of paper on which he was about to draw.

This time she couldn't stem the tide of fear which shook her. 'He means to kill me,' she murmured. She held on to the bed for support. Grimly she battled her way back to the surface of her screaming mind.

There was an ominous rumbling overhead as a sheet of snow pitched off the roof. The thaw was gathering momentum.

8

'Do keep still.' His voice was sharp.

She hadn't been aware she moved. Her neck ached. The morning sun was gone, and now a fine grey light defined the room, clarifying and isolating the objects, one from another. They seemed suspended in space, she thought, their relationships destroyed. She wondered whether this was a measure of her alienation from the room, from him, from what he was doing to her.

He had arranged her with obsessive care. 'The hair must half-shadow the face,' he told her. He didn't say 'your' hair, 'your' face. 'The legs must be half drawn up to the stomach, the hands clasped loosely about them.' He had become impatient with her. 'The limbs are too stiff.' Well, she was embarrassed. And he hadn't asked her to pose in the nude for him. Was she just a little bit annoyed about that? Was her figure so awful? Augustus John would have stripped her down. But not him, oh no, not Leo. He was only interested in hidden things, unobserved realities. 'They are limbs not palings!' He got quite enraged. Some sugar-paper was clipped to a drawing-board. On the table was one of Dermott's cylinders of pencils.

He pushed her foot, rearranged her fingers and then went off to the window to contemplate the smudging landscape. He lit a cigarette and left her to it. She struggled with her embarrassment, her spurts of anger. Why should she parade herself for him? But deep down she was flattered. He was putting her on paper, wasn't he? She might even go on a wall and stare impassively into the room, the way portraits do. 'Well, that's it.' He turned to survey her. 'You've fallen into it at last', he said and went over to pick up the drawing-board.

'What are you after?' She had been curious.

'Half-curled up and defensive, but a bit defiant too. Impossible to describe, really, your pose. What Dermott would have called "the language of the body". He could be a pretentious bastard. How he did enjoy being the big talent, the *one*.'

Leo had now been working for thirty minutes. At first his pencil had moved very quickly and through half the sugar-paper, sheet after sheet being ripped off and left at his feet. Now he was working slowly and she felt, with painful concentration. Was he engaged in a battle with her, the paper, or himself?

'Do keep still.' His voice was sharp.

These words every now and then punctuated the silence, beads suspended on invisible threads. The silence had its own quality. Not a quiet quiet, but a tenseness sometimes bordering on desperation—not a quiet quiet at all. She couldn't see his face, because he had posed her looking away from him. Deliberately? She could only see some of the wall, some of the objects on Dermott's desk objects bereft of shadows, of anything that seemed to commit them to the room, to each other. Is this what disintegration is really like, she wondered—nothing dramatic at all, just a boring disconnection? It was her neck which ached the most, half-twisted away from him, supporting her head in such a way that not even a hair should fall beyond its present boundary in space.

Hadn't she read somewhere that artists chatted pleasantly to their victims as they drew them? He probably wasn't a real artist at all. He had said he taught at art school, but why should she believe him? He was a liar, wasn't he? He seemed to think that the truth was only a convention he needed to adhere to when it suited him. Even if he were an artist, he would probably draw her with one eye and a hand coming out of her head. How boring! What a travesty of vision! But there was this terrible silence, wasn't there? He and the paper were certainly involved in something.

'Do keep still.'

Christ! She wasn't moving an inch. Her muscles would soon reach screaming point. Why not get off this damned chair and jump about? The idea thrilled her. Smash the silence. But the thought of him, the pencil, the transferring of her image on to paper, kept her still. It was almost as if she were taking part in a magic rite. His magic, not hers. Did she have any powers at all?

And suddenly she remembered the fire in the cellar and something about the hose. What was it? They couldn't use the hose-pipe ... why? She was badly frightened. It was important to remember. She must remember exactly what he said.

Now she was frozen into the pose he had given her.

'O.K., you can relax. I've got the line down. But try to keep as near the pose as you can. Funny, I do other people. But not family. Not my mother. In particular, not her. It's like trying to capture the sea. Each time I look it's different. A new world.'

He had taken the bowl from her at the top of the cellar steps ... she had picked up the buckets ...

'There was always the sea at home, of course. It gave the town an extra dimension. A way out. A way of escape. An open door to the prison. Of course, you never had to use it ... its being there was enough, all that horizon, all that sky ... Don't frown.'

'What?'

'You are frowning.'

She was deep in thought. 'A hose. We need a hose.' Yes. She had said something like that. What an exasperating room! Everything picked for it and nothing belonging.

'So cosy,' he said. 'With all those tea-shops and old people. So soothing.'

'Why don't you go back there,' she shouted. Stupid man. What was it? What had he said—'Haven't got a hose?' Yes. That was it. 'In barn. Used.' Oh, my God.

'I think I will. Go back there. I don't like this place. I don't like the feel of it. Grey, grim … covered in its own muck and proud of it.'

The hose seemed to squeeze her very spirit.

'Well, what do you think?'

'What?'

'This damned place. What do you think?'

'I've got a headache. How much longer will you be?'

'Not long now. Will you smoke?'

'No.'

'Perhaps somewhere up the coast a bit. Quieter.'

'What about your wife?' Her voice was low and sombre. She was flexing her fingers. 'What about her, Leo?' The knife, she remembered, was in her pocket.

'My wife?'

'What about her, Leo?'

He was silent and then he smiled, a sudden sweetness in his face. 'She won't mind.'

'She—'

'No, no. She sees things my way, now.'

She had ceased to listen to him. Her mind ran in rivulets—her fear, her sense of being ridiculous, of construing the grotesque out of thin air … And yet and yet. What could he have done with the hose? What would he need a hose for in the middle of a blizzard?

'Of course, she wanted to get wed. She was thirty-three, Jane. She didn't want to be a "Miss" all her life. Why? Christ! No one could accuse her of being an old maid. Far from it!'

'It's all right being a hell-raiser in your twenties. When you're on the road to forty its pathetic.' Her voice was sharper than she intended.

'She wasn't forty,' he shouted.

'Perhaps that was her reasoning.'

'No!'

'But you think she didn't love you?' She was mocking him.

'Did I say that? Did I ever say that?'

'You implied it.' She was increasingly sharp, destructive.

'I don't know,' he muttered. He had retreated further from her. 'Perhaps she thought she could love me. Perhaps she would have if—'

'What?'

'... tall and big and warm and easy. Oh God. Oh my God. I thought I had it made. I thought I did. All that luscious hair. Rapunzel. That's who her hair reminded me of.'

'Climbing up her hair ...' Unaccountably Christie began to shiver.

'Hothouse. Everything she used on herself smelled of this or that, and she was lavish, she was lavish in everything—creams, lip-sticks, huge bubble-baths. Like loving a pot-pourri. Almost asphyxiated.'

'So you did love her.'

'Oh, she wasn't all violets and roses. There were other things she liked to wallow in. She wasn't particular about housework for one.'

'I thought artists didn't mind about dirty cups and things.'

'I'm like Dermott. I like order. I like things clean and straight. There's enough chaos about without it creeping under your front door.'

Did his wife ... Jane ... did the luscious Jane dangle from the hose-pipe in the barn? I could go mad, she thought. If I went mad these imaginings would have no significance, because they would have no connection with reality. I could go deep into myself and quietly go bloody raving mad. I could do that.

121

'Shoes.'

'What?'

'So feminine, but because she was lame she always wore flat shoes. Great strong clod-hopping, humping things. Straightlaced. Masculine.' He laughed, suddenly, joyously. 'Lovely! Beautiful! Women never realise how exciting the unexpected can be.'

'It's getting colder.' She was beginning to shiver in earnest. 'Cold. Colder.'

'I wonder—'

'Cold. Don't you think?'

'Oh, yes. Lace-ups. Lovely lace-ups!'

She broke pose and turned to him. He stared at her, shocked. She had a feeling he was ceasing to see her as separate but as something projected from himself.

He didn't like being confronted with her alienness, her animosity. He didn't like being reminded she existed at all. And she caught hold of his shock and felt it, too. 'I'm here,' she wanted to shout. 'I'm me. I'm not Jane, or your first wife, or any of the women who people your imagination!' But she said nothing. She was aware now of his aggression. He would, he could, stamp her out. But his voice was soft. 'I've not finished.' The light on his glasses made his eyes into great underwater pebbles.

'Oh.' She was bewildered. She wondered what she should do now.

'I haven't finished the drawing. Not quite.' Though his voice was quiet, she knew *he* wasn't. He roared.

'Yes.' Her confusion grew. What was she doing here in this room at The Bield—in all this steely light, an object among so many hostile objects?

'Take up the pose. Take up the pose, please.'

'Yes.'

'I've not finished yet.'

'Leo.'

'Yes?'

But there was no point in appealing to him. It had

gone. It had all gone. The sea had come in and washed the words off the sand. Slowly, reluctantly, she found her way back into the pose.

I mustn't play his games, she thought, alarmed. I mustn't take part in his rituals. It will be the end of me.

But she felt tired, tired of fighting against impressions, feelings, shadows. What real shred of evidence was there to support her monstrous construction of events? Where were the weapons, the bodies? Where was the reality of it all? Even the objects on Dermott's desk didn't look real. They had lost their meaning. They were tones of light and dark, a jumble of patterns she couldn't decipher.

He said, working again. 'There's something quite awful about The Bield. All that winter in her stones. There's nothing like that in the south. Nothing quite like it there. All this jazzing up Dermott's done ... all this converting ... Well, you can't convert an old bitch's evil soul, can you?'

Christie thought of The Bield she had known as a child, The Bield for ever and ever, solid, strong, not changing. She and her father coming off Rake Top, down by the old quarry shafts and the drift of bluebell smells tinged with an odour of sulphur which never quite left the valley air. The Bield always lay below them, growing through their consciousness, pointing homewards. The path tumbled by the barn to the road, back to Swiss rolls and boiled ham for tea, back to washing on the lines, stalking cats with glittering eyes and the blue television lights twinkling through windows. It was so exciting, the setting out, the coming back. It was always the same, even when she was older and moved through the hills alone. 'Rake Top is a special place,' her father had told her. 'An old place where some valley people have always come. Proper valley people. Our people. Why, in my grandfather's youth ...' and he had looked at her and laughed and said no more. He didn't need to say anything. Rake Top dominated all the valley churches. Its roots spread deep and silently in people's minds. Valley people didn't need to talk of Rake Top any more than Sunday dinner.

'But I think I'll go back to the South,' Leo went on. 'Some people spend all their lives escaping from the scenes of their youth, but I'm not one of those. Obviously not. It's all right. I'm finished.'

Now that Christie could, at last, break pose, she didn't. To do so was to move on, and she felt threatened by all this moving on—not so much moving on as down, scuttling and scampering until she reached her blind alley and there was no escape. No way through. No continuance.

'I've said it's O.K. All right, I've finished. Stretch, relax. It's done.'

Very reluctantly she unwound herself and rubbed her joints. 'Is it good?'

He studied his work and her in silence. 'Yes,' he said, at length. 'Have I got one eye and a breast hanging off my nose?'

He snorted with sudden laughter. 'No.'

'I'm glad about that. At least there's that ...' and she exercised a leg. 'My ankle's still a bit sore. Can I see it? Can I see myself?'

'Yes.'

She got up. She didn't really want to go near him, and yet she wanted to see his drawing of her. The light had grown dull. The room was shadowing in at the corners, so that, instead of a rectangle, they seemed to move in a circle. He had put the drawing on Dermott's desk and turned to the window. 'Christ,' he yawned. 'It's going to rain. That will soon clear it. The snow.'

She picked up the drawing. She saw herself curled, defensive, shadowed in her hair. The drawing was good, the likeness exact, but she was disappointed. It's certainly how I am, she thought, exactly how I am. The disappointment still lingered. What she was and what she wanted to be seemed two irreconcilable poles. Had he drawn her to warn, to show her what a tentative, half-finished thing she was, incapable of standing up to him, to anything? 'Well, you've caught me, yes,' she said flatly.

'I think I have.' He yawned again.

'You've caught me all right.'

'You don't approve?'

'I feel cheated,' she said truculently.

'Cheated?' He was surprised.

'That this is all I am.'

He turned to her. He was amused. 'You are lovely. In your own way. Some animals live in the sun, out and about and full of beans. Others are night creatures. They like the dark, the shadows and the shade. Eyes in the depth of the undergrowth. You remind me of one of those. A creature of darkness.'

She shivered. 'You're so fanciful. I'm a pots-and-pans lady who makes her living by stamping library books!'

He yawned again. 'That's your *role*. Not what you *are*. No one is mundane. Being part of life, being part of death ... we must all be heroes, don't you think? God, I'm tired. It's being up all night. That bloody fire. I think I'll go upstairs and have a sleep. It'll be some time yet before we can get out of this place. It'll need a few hours of rain to wash enough of the snow away for us to get through. Can I have the drawing?'

'Aren't I to have it?'

'No.'

'But why not?' She was unaccountably distressed.

'I want a reminder,' he said softly. 'A reminder of you. I might forget you. That wouldn't do, would it? I don't want to forget what you look like.' He smiled as he took the drawing. 'You should be flattered.'

He left her stranded in the room. She heard him climb the stairs, she heard the door at the top of the landing click shut. She didn't know why, but she felt uneasy, suspicious. She thought it would have been safer to have him under her eye. Did he, she wondered, see life as some improbable drama and himself as a hero? Or even a god? Not an ordinary art teacher with an ordinary wife who wore lace-up shoes? Was The Bield his fantasy and had he assigned her a role in his dreams?

Suddenly rain was on the window. She darted across. The landscape was changing. It really *was* changing. Soon she would be home. Tomorrow would be like all her days. The Bield would be over. Relief came to her— strong, sweet, heady, releasing, like the scent of July phlox. The rain came down harder.

At the other end of the farmyard, bounding her vision, was the barn, an underwater cliff now that it was raining so hard. The dog had quietly come to her and was sitting beside her. She looked down when she felt its presence. Its amber eyes waited on her with the infinite patience of a serene being. 'I'll go to it. I'll go to the barn. I will know. One way and another I will know. I'll get all of this out of my system once and for all.'

But she would need a key to get in. Where was it? His anorak hung half on a chair. She walked quickly over to it, standing uncertain, listening. The house was quiet. There was no sound from him. But what if she did find something? What if, at last, her imaginings became real? She would somehow fight her way through the snow, fight her way to the road. After all, it was raining hard now. The snow was melting quickly. And if the barn were bare? She would come back to the house and wait until more snow was washed away, an hour or two perhaps. After all, why not?

She touched the sleeve of the anorak. Her fingers frantically scrabbled about a pocket. Her eye was on the door. But, of course, he wouldn't suddenly appear. There would be sound of him first.

She tugged out a bunch of keys and then extracted a solitary one. It was large, its handle slightly bent, a

Victorian key, though The Bield was much older than that. 'Well,' she said to the dog. 'Oh dear.'

She put her jacket on, dropping the key in her pocket as she went into the hall, and the dog followed. She looked about for something to put on her head and her eye caught the triangular lattice of hat-rack above her head. She took down Dermott's ratting cap. Fear whispered along her spine. A dead man's hat? She jammed the cap over her ears. Her fingers went down to the left-hand pocket of her jacket. Fingers curled over the handle of the knife she had honed. She stood quite still. She was breathing deeply. 'God,' she said between her teeth. Her courage had failed her. The chill gloom seemed to come off the corners of the hall and mesh her into the fabric of the farmhouse. 'God!' She burst forward and wrenched open the front door. The dog went with her.

She hurried into her original diggings. They were slurping and moving in the rain. The whole wet landscape was in motion. She could hear it slithering and shuddering. She loved it. She loved it when the earth talked to her. How she would miss that when she died! She cast a surreptitious look back at The Bield. It lay rain-curtained and quiet. She could discern no observing eyes. She was in his diggings now and rain was running down her neck. To her left were the other diggings and the coat, flattened and glinting like an oil spillage. Of the glove and its melting fingers there was no sign.

The barn rose in the wet like some great whale, and she touched its hoary side to steady herself. She could feel no one observing her. Her mind tried to penetrate the stones of the farmhouse, but the walls shielded him. Still, nothing attracted her alarm. She swung back to the barn. 'Here we go then.' But the dog wasn't there to hear her. It didn't like the rain.

Her numbed fingers rattled the key in the lock, but she could get no purchase. She began to shake. A sudden gust of wind lifted Dermott's cap off her head, and it was flung high on a freshening burst of rain. She took a firmer grip on the key. The door fell away from her, crashing back on its hinges. 'Christ!' Her knees buckled with alarm. She clutched hold of the streaming stonework, and the door began to come towards her. She held it at arm's length, sniffing and peering into the angle of lightened gloom, but she could discover nothing.

As she edged herself into the barn, the widening light pointed across uneven but clean stone flags. Dermott again! She might have guessed that all would be neat and tidy. The air in the barn was grey-green and so piercingly damp that she might have been in an underwater cave. How foolish not to have brought a torch. She was frightened, yet elated, and again she had a strong sense of being part of a ritual—of performing in some required pattern.

The shape of the barn was becoming clearer to her now. The grey-green darkness lightened where a small window overlooked the farmyard, barred and covered with chicken mesh wire.

High up a loft ran three-quarters of the barn's length, its weight supported by a series of wooden uprights. These central poles with their triangular tops gave the barn a crypt-like appearance, though she supposed that they supported nothing more religious than hay. There was no ladder up. Between the uprights, in the centre of the floor space, a ledge, a platform, rose. The newness of the wood was pale in the darkness. She frowned. A platform? It was so out of place, so unexpected. Musicians, she thought. Dermott must have had parties in this bone-chilling place. She looked but could find no trace of electric lights, but on three of the uprights paraffin lamps dangled. Her gaze focused again on the platform. There was something on it, but at this distance she couldn't guess what, something low and long and shadowy, something greyish white. If she investigated further she would have to let the barn door shut. She was loth to do that. Why hadn't she brought a torch!

Looking about her, she saw a bucket and mop by the entrance of the barn. Noisily she edged the bucket to her and wedged the door, which looked none too secure. She began to fill the bucket with the pebbles that were strewn about the barn's doorway. It steadied.

She looked out again, towards the house. The rain was coming down so hard now that the outline of the farmhouse was obscured. It had gone into the mountain, its menace magnified by its invisibility. She shuddered and turned.

Her journey to the centre of the barn was now partially lit. Everything was tidy; not even a rat seemed to startle the shadows. But she became more and more frightened. Her hair bristled. 'Oh, Jesus,' she murmured as she swayed on her feet.

Her hands steadied on the knife in her pocket. She felt unreal; she was threading her way through a dream. The door scraped behind her. She hadn't put enough pebbles in the bucket. She could go back. After all, there was nothing in the barn. 'There's something on the platform.' She spoke aloud. But even her words seemed to lose their reality, and sighed in the barn, as nebulous as shifting blasts of draught. The bucket rattled. That at least was real.

She looked at the platform. It had certainly not long been made. She was now so near that she could smell the raw wood. It was sheet, sheeting. Did it cover instruments? But who would leave them in a damp barn? She couldn't say why, she didn't know why, but the rhythms of *In Memorium* moved in her head and with them trickles of Pre-Raphaelite paintings, of endless shrouded ladies in endless misty lilies sailing in dead water. 'Oh God. Oh Christ! I ought to get out of this place. Go.' The bucket set up a merry rattle. The door closed further.

As she went on, she came to the bottom of three crude wooden steps which led up to the platform. A wine-coloured stain impregnated the top step.

Even in this cold there was a buzz of fly, and an occasional wafting of a faint, musky, sweet smell she couldn't name: a fetid-hole smell, a death smell. She was surprised to feel silent tears on her cheeks.

She mounted the crude steps, which squealed beneath her foot, and looked down. They were both wrapped in sheeting. The folds were finely calculated, bands of light, shade and impenetrable black. Green hose piping held the shrouds in place. By the breast the piping was garlanded with green sugar-paper. It should have been earth things, she realised, leaves and grasses, but they were sunk under snow. The woman's gold-coloured hair was flowing, glinting green in the greenish light. It sprayed over her breast in lines of shocking beauty. They were already beyond time and space, in a dimension truly their own—like a painting, she thought.

But they were real, real dead people. They weren't effigies. They were corpses.

All that terrible passion brought to order, those savagely murdered people organised in death so that not one speck of blood sullied their funeral garb. Image within beautifully controlled image, the whole focused on wide-open eyes which stared into perpetual darkness.

The image grew and grew inside Christie's mind, detail on indelible detail.

They lay side by side, but nowhere did they touch. It was as though a ruler had been used to divide him off from her. Their jaws had been firmly taped with sticking plaster, the plaster intricately binding, like gadroon edging on silver. Her toes, under the sheeting, were clearly discernible.

The weight of image began to push at Christie, began to shift, to topple her. She crashed off the platform. The bucket danced. The barn door was almost closed now.

She lay face down on the flag floor, but her eyes were open, staring into nothing, like those of Dermott and his mistress. Her mind was clear, though, her hearing sharp. She lay in the briny womb of the barn, unable to move, but each particle of her shockingly aware of everything. The door crashed shut. She waited. She heard him turn the key in the lock.

9

Her back was against the wall, her head bowed into her lap. She had been crying for a long time and she would go on crying, a low, monotonous, endlessly repeating grief. She was sorry for the dead on the platform, she was sorry for the mountains of dead from whom she had sprung, but above all, oh Christ, she was sorry for herself. So brief were the hazes of quivering summers, rain-pelting winters, a squeal of life in cold, everlasting dark. How would her dying flesh feel? She had no doubt he would kill her. He would kill her and wrap her up and make a pretty parcel of her. By tomorrow she would be gone.

And so she grieved on and on, the regrets rustling and sleek with life in the undergrowth of her mind, a myriad eyes on myriad worlds.

She had dragged herself from the centre of the floor to this inconspicuous corner of the barn. It had been a time-consuming, laborious business. She slithered and flapped like a fish on rock. Her body didn't work, or worked in all the wrong sequences. She was trapped in its uselessness, her uselessness, a victim as surely as a sea creature left by a receding tide.

Gradually she became aware of the noise she was making. Gradually she felt the texture of the stone which supported her back and she began to discern, too, the bulking shapes of the barn. But she decided not to put by her grief: it was a retreat, a warmth, a consolation.

Her eye sought out the door, away in the far corner,

and her tears began to dry as she waited for him. She saw him clearly, his halo of hair, his glasses, his crumpled corduroy trousers; she saw him as a man, and she saw him too as something endlessly dark, endlessly evil, a death-figure of such gigantic proportions that she almost fainted. What would he do? How would he do it? How long would it take? And she waited, dry-eyed now, her grieving over. What would she do when he opened the door? She couldn't say. She didn't know. She didn't know herself.

Her shoulders straightened. She wanted a good view. She needed to raise her head a little more to get a really good view. It was so dark now—darker and darker, like Maureen's lounge-diner lifetimes ago.

She felt him near, felt almost choked by his smothering presence. He was very, very near. Her eyes strained through the gloom. The door was firmly shut. But he was near, near.

Turning to the distant window, she saw a monstrous shadow head, dark gloom on light gloom imprinted on a rectangle on the barn floor. The head was moving, moving. It was seeking. He couldn't see her. She flattened herself further back into the wall. She was watching the window now, watching the head small and bobbing.

Her breath began to grind, as if squeezed between two stones. She laboured over wracking fright. The head was stilled. Had he seen her now, clinging and agonized against the back wall of the barn?

She heard his feet, slushing as if through tidal waters. She heard the key in the lock. Each rattle separated out in her mind and stayed with her, echoing on and on. She shut her eyes. He was coming. He was here. The door was opened and there were his steps, distant at first but now louder, bouncy, brisk.

'Well,' he said, his voice shining and song-like. 'Just like I first found you. In the wardrobe. All curled up. Like a snail ...' and he chuckled.

She looked up at him, as he stood within easy reach of her, his body blocking out the dying light from the barn door, his glasses pushed into his springing, curling hair. He was examining her minutely, but she couldn't see his eyes. His face was too deeply in shadow. In his hand was a bottle. Had he been drinking? But his words were diamond bright, cut cleanly from his mind.

She felt herself responding to his alien presence. Her body was still shut up in fright, but a coldness was forming in her being, and from here she watched him and herself, acutely aware, not seeming to scheme but scheming.

'I knew you would find them. You kept poking and prying in the wrong directions, not at all sure—not at all sure you wanted to find them. But in the end I knew you'd come to them. People are so very keen on the worst. A focal point. An explaining point. In a humdrum endlessly trivial life I knew, in the end, you'd come ...'

'You did murder them.'

'Yes. Yes, I did. Before you came.'

'Yes. Of course. Oh my God.'

'He was first.'

'Christ.' The words splintered in her head.

'I hadn't intended to do it. I came ... well, I don't quite know why I came. I knew Jane was seeing him. Having it off still ... never stopped, probably, except to take a taxi to the Register Office to marry me.'

'I always knew. I always knew. Since I first stumbled in through the front door of The Bield. Oh ... Christ!'

'Yes, well it was pretty unbearable. Knowing he was having her ... and the pair of them watching. Watching me for some reaction. They knew I was on to them. After all, the whole bloody muck-heap town knew. They were all watching. Watching to see what I would do.'

'Why did she marry you!'

'*He* wouldn't marry *her*.' And then Jane and I met ... while she was on holiday. Perhaps she really thought it would be all right. She could make a break. Perhaps she really believed that. And she was no spring chicken any more. Not that that mattered to anyone but her. It is like saying the wind is getting middle-aged. I—' He stopped.

Christie knew then that not only had he loved her but he still did, still would, no matter the name of the woman he took to his bed. She was aware of his tragedy, and yet she was completely untouched by it.

'Of course, you understand, don't you?' His voice was gentle. 'You understand it all, Christie. That's what's so remarkable about you. When you stop worrying about your own muddles and turn to other people you have this ... empathy.'

'You didn't put that in your drawing of me,' she shouted.

'How bitter you sound! Does it matter? How can a little thing like that matter?'

'It does.' And she couldn't put into words, she wouldn't say that if he had let himself give all of her to the paper he couldn't so easily plan to kill her. Her body felt a new surge of panic. But the cold, separate part of her was still growing.

She was watching, she was waiting: she didn't know for what. He let his glasses drop back into place. He was rocking on his feet, nervous. Excited?

'You can't get away with it.'

'What?' He was nonplussed.

'All this. In the barn. It's no good. You'll get caught. They'll have you in no time. No time at all.'

He smiled. 'Will they? Will they now? I'll just quietly go away. Be a different man. Disappear. I'll lock all this inside me. It will be a hoard of jewels. Something I can take out and examine from time to time. In secret.'

'You—'

'Well, you must know, Christie. You seem to understand most things. You must know how it is with me. Now. First—well, him—Dermott. He was in anger.

He came towards me. The bastard was going to thump me. He'd been out for logs for the fire and was coming through the back door when he saw me. He dropped the logs and was going to thump me one! I got the knife from the rack behind me. God, I was scared. Scared of him. I got hold of his meat knife. Sharp point at the end. I didn't mean to kill him, but there it was. The kitchen is so small. Narrow. Couldn't miss him. Easy to stick a knife in him. Just happened. I didn't intend to kill him. Not at all. It just happened. Jane must have heard the racket, because I heard her running down the stairs. She was shouting. She ... well, she was for pleasure, Christie. I was enjoying myself so much. My God ... it was fantastic.'

'You enjoyed it?' She was helpless before him, not wanting to understand, but understanding too well.

'Jane didn't realise Dermott was dead. She thought he was just hurt. She ran to telephone for an ambulance. I followed her into the hall. And suddenly, well ... our eyes met. And though we didn't speak she knew. She knew then, all right. She knew I'd killed him. She knew I was going to kill her. Of course, I didn't kill her immediately. It was all too good for that. I took my time. Sliced through the telephone wire first. Before I sliced her. Just so she'd know, know how sharp the knife was. Know how it was going to be. Me and her together.'

'You played games!'

'Yes. Oh yes!'

'The blood,' she whispered. 'The blood on the rug. And the chair upturned.'

'Not much mess, really. Not a lot of mess, considering. She didn't die at once. Dermott died almost immediately. But not her. She sort of staggered about a bit. And then when she sank to the floor I took her in my arms. She knew, of course. She said: "This is it. This is it, eh?" And she let it come to her. Didn't fight it. She had all the courage in the world.' Silent tears ran down his cheeks. He made no attempt to stop them.

'So you're sorry, after all.'

'No. No. I'm not. I'm not sorry. It was perfect. I'd created those perfect moments. She never blamed me. She seemed to admire me. She made me feel a man. She took it all, and at the end I held her close. It was perfect.'

'You—'

'The barn was for her. A tribute. I wanted her to be found in beauty. I even put him by her side. I did it for her. It's superb, isn't it?'

She shivered.

'It's superb. The best thing I've ever done.'

'Leo!'

'What?'

'You are—'

'What?'

'Are you crazy?'

He considered. 'No. I was very tidy. Ordered. I cleaned myself up first and then the house. It was hard work, the house, and I hadn't quite time to do everything. But I did it well, considering ... I brought them out here. Dragged them on Dermott's coat. She rolled off. I suppose the glove must have spilled out of the pocket. I carried them the rest of the way. I did everything properly, you know. I hadn't time to clean the things I'd been wearing, of course. I bundled them up. It all took a long time. I did everything properly.'

'Leo—'

'... A very long time. I didn't think of the snow. I didn't think I'd get snowed up in the barn. That was frightening. Being alone with them when I'd finished my work.' He touched the corduroy pants. 'These are Dermott's. He was older than me.'

'Older?' She was bewildered.

'Much older. Yet Jane still seemed to prefer him. Except at the end. At the end it was all different. I burned the things that had to be burnt—my things. I burned them in the cellar. In that fire. Before you or anyone else had a chance to find them.'

'You were in the nude,' she whispered.

He suddenly laughed, a great, billowing, liberating sound. 'Diversions. Oh, it's such fun, Christie!'

'You really did. You really enjoyed it all. I couldn't quite believe it when you said about her … pleasure … enjoying killing her. But you did, didn't you? You must be mad.'

'Why do you keep going on about that? Men kill in war and some soldiers enjoy doing it. Man is a killer. I am a killer. It took some getting used to, that idea. It took a while for me to make up my mind. There was you, for instance. You weren't involved with their mucky mess. You just stumbled into it all … but when I really thought about it, I knew.'

'Knew what?'

His voice was soft. 'I won't even remember your face in a month's time.'

She felt her hair lift on her scalp. Her legs pushed hard against the floor as she levered herself up to face him.

'I started all this as Leo Brinsley, a bit of a failed artist. A bit of a failed teacher whose missus was having a bit on the side. I'd never have found out who I really was if I hadn't stuck that knife at a lucky point in Dermott's hide. I'm a killer, Christie. That's what puts me together. It truly does.' She saw he was shining with excitement.

'Well, that's it. That's all. The truth about me.' The hand that held the bottle quivered. 'Ah,' he bellowed. 'I feel bloody marvellous.'

She was transfixed. There's nothing I can do, she thought, nothing to do. There's no way out. I'm not a person any more. Is it the bottle? Will he batter me with that? She found herself screaming: 'You can't! You can't!'

'No, I couldn't make up my mind about you. Not at first. I thought … well, if you didn't find them I'd let you go … but that was silly. I wasn't thinking straight. All the shock, the excitement of it all! Silly. The corpses would be found and you'd tell them I'd been here. But you had nothing to do with it. You were incidental. It was nothing to do with you ... you shouldn't be punished for something that wasn't your fault. That's conventional morality. Conditioning. Hell, I don't have any morals. I can do what I like. I'm free, I really am. I'm bloody well free of it all now. Of course, it took a while for that to sink in. Christie ... Christie, my love ... I shan't be guilty about you. Do you realise? I won't even remember your face in a month's time.'

'You're an animal! There's nothing left of you. You're just an animal.'

His face glittered. 'I'm a god. I'm a god. That's what I am. That's what I am, love. Don't you know that yet? Don't you feel it?'

'Leo!'

'I'm a god.' His exultant voice went on and on, rushing from him, words exploding, breaking about her in a great torrent. His hands flew about, the bottle gleaming. His legs pumped out a jerky dance, a war dance. That's it, she thought. He's intoxicating himself. He's celebrating. He's celebrating my death!

'Of course, I will remember. I will remember you now. I put it down. I drew you on that paper. All your loveliness. You are lovely, you know. But you don't move me. You don't touch me. Not like Jane. Not like my wife did. You have something, though ... soft and furry and big-eyed, something vulnerable about you. And I'm the big bad wolf, dearie!' His laughter burst upwards, spurting out like a great fountain.

She couldn't move. She was hypnotised by him, his movement, his endless sounds, the great furnace of his power.

'But I'm not an animal. I'm not an animal, you know. You're wrong about that. I've got some pity for you. After all, you've done nothing wrong. It's not your fault.

You just stumbled into my little den, stumbled in on us.' He thrust the bottle into her hand. 'That's for you. That's my gift to you, Christie, love. Nirvana. After all, you see, I do have pity. I'm not an animal. No, no, not at all.'

She stared at him, horrified.

'For you. For you. For you! Drink it. Sweet dreams. You'll never know it happened, dearie. Never see death steal up. See, I do have pity. I'm arranging things nicely for you. And then I'll just go away. Disappear. Fade into the masses. They won't find Leo Brinsley. He's already disappeared. He doesn't exist any more.'

'You won't find it easy. It's not so easy. It can't be! They'll catch you.'

'Nonsense, Christie. You know you're talking rubbish. They won't. I was going to add you—add you to their scene, you know. But you don't belong. You'd spoil my work. You belong to the mountain. See. I've thought about you. I've really thought about you. I know where you belong. To the mountain.'

'You're stark, staring mad!' she screamed.

'I'm not,' he howled.

'You—'

But his bubbling excitement had suddenly cut itself off. The heated planes of his face grew cold. He seemed, she thought, to shrivel. He said brusquely: 'Well, I've got work to do. I won't be all that long.' He turned and hurried out of the barn. She heard the door slam. The key snapped in the lock.

She ran to the window and craned her neck round to see him. A spade was propped against the wall. Shouldering it, he trudged through the rapidly dissolving snow up the rain-shrouded mountain-side. She knew what he was doing. He had gone to dig her grave.

Staring at his retreating figure, she flung the bottle on the flags, and the noise echoed in the icy shadows of the barn. The liquid escaped into the pores of the stone, its going staining a widening patch of floor. He would be

140

angry. He would be angry with her. She was breaking up the ritual: his ritual, his patterning of her death. It would be the worse for her when he got his fingers on her. Sweat made her gleam in the ever-deepening gloom. How much time had she got? How long did it take to dig a grave? She thought of the hard, unyielding earth on the hard, unyielding mountain. It wouldn't be easy. He would need all his strength.

She looked round the barn. A feeling of hopelessness swept over her. There was no way out. She looked up at the loft, which covered three-quarters of the building's roof space. Surely there was a window, or was it a door, up there? On the east wall? She had seen hay being hoisted through it, hadn't she?

She tried to picture herself coming down from Rake Top, coming home with her father. She saw the path which twisted down past the farm, she saw the barn below her. And surely some cart drawn up and fodder of some kind being hoisted through an opening on the barn's upper storey.

She looked at the loft. There were no steps anywhere. No means of getting up. But there must be a way up, she thought. If I'm right surely there's a way up. Could the old farmer have used a ladder? But there was no ladder in the barn now, only the cleaning materials by the door, the platform, the corpses. But there was a central upright where the loft ended and the barn soared upwards to its roof. Could she shin up that? At school she had never managed to climb the ropes. 'I'll break my neck,' she said aloud, and she laughed grimly.

She investigated the upright. It looked very sturdy. How did one begin? She mustn't just stand around, she must hurry. If he knew the area he'd just stuff her down one of the old mine shafts. It would be years before she was found. She made for the bucket by the cleaning materials and upturned it at the bottom of the wooden column, gazing at the loft. It seemed so high up. She clambered on the bucket and raised her arms, gripping the beam and then folding her legs round it. Her muscles began to pull, but clumsily she managed to shunt herself upwards.

A sharp, inward vision of him shouldering the spade came into her mind. Her body froze, her numbed limbs slithered from the upright and she crashed to the floor. His long, frizzy hair had touched the shaft of the spade. The blade had glistened dully in the rain. She was crying in terror.

She pulled herself off the floor. Tears were still running down her cheeks as she clambered back on the bucket. She began again. Up and up she grimly pushed herself. She couldn't say whether the agony she felt was fright or strain. But she went up and up, her bleeding hands trembling as they reached the loft, her shoulder muscles twitching weakly. But she had to drag herself over the lip of the loft. She pushed her body higher and higher on the column, and then suddenly, terrifyingly, she flung herself forward and lay in the darkness listening to the tumultuous sound of her heart, her limbs shaking. The cold separateness she had felt the beginnings of when he was in the barn with her had now forged itself through anger into an implacable hardness. She would kill him. She could kill him. 'Leo, Leo,' she whispered, her mind suddenly reverting to his naked image illuminated by the fire in the cellar. Her terror was momentarily gone and he dwelled in her blood, a heavy, sweet heat.

There was no window. But there must be, she thought. The cart? The hoisting hay seen through a lowering evening light? Had she imagined it? Was the image wish-fulfilment? But she even remembered what her father was wearing. Rough and checked, an absurd Norfolk jacket: 'Lord of the council house cats!' The ever-biting edge of her mother's misery came back. Yes, yes, there was certainly something. A door?

In a corner she heard a skittering, and the hairs at the

142

nape of her neck stirred. A rat? The rain drummed quietly over her head. She felt her mind begin to melt at the edges. Shakily she pulled herself to her feet and began to explore the icy barn walls. Then she dimly apprehended it, in the east end of the barn, the door of her childhood, no bigger than a small window and bolted firmly across. Down on her knees she tackled the bolt. It was rusted in. She tried again, pushing as hard as she could, but it wouldn't budge. 'Jesus,' she muttered. 'Jesus.' How long had it been since Leo left her?

'... sweet dreams. You'll never know it happened, dearie. Never know that death stole up on you.'

She thumped frantic frustrated hands on the floor. Aware of her pain, she steadied herself, breathing deeply, ever more quietly.

Wedging her foot against the short handle of the bolt, she began to kick, booting the bolt with mounting fury. The iron squealed. It shot back and she fell over.

As she took the latch in her hand, she saw another bolt at the top of the door. She groaned. This one wasn't stuck so fast, but she was aware of the rushing away of time. She pushed, wriggled and teased it, and very slowly it jerked down the shaft. She opened the door. It fell off a hinge and drunkenly hit the wall.

The smudging white of snow was absorbing the wet night like ink running into blotting paper. A wind was up. The rain carried in unexpected, violent gusts. The door cracked into her, and she shuffled nearer the opening, holding it back with her free hand.

She peered further out. She couldn't see the farm from here. The buildings lay at rough right angles, but the barn was set further back into the mountain, and all she could see was a low stone wall and beyond it a field which led upwards to Rake Top itself. At the right of this field was a public footpath, the one she had walked as a child with her father, but this was obliterated by snow, which still gathered deep about the base of the stone walls.

At first she thought it was the wind cracking in a tree. But there was a steady, slushing sound also. He was coming back, coming down Rake Top. She was too petrified to move. She sat frozen in the miniature doorway, in plain sight.

Seeing the stone wall move, she realised that it was Leo climbing over the wall. A stone broke loose and tumbled into the snow. He steadied himself with a thrust-down spade and was over the wall and coming directly to the barn. The snow was no more than ankle deep now. He marched through it with his head back, the spade lying on his shoulder like a warrior's pike. He was dark against the darkening slush and he gleamed rainily, a triumphal figure, an avenging angel.

'Onward Christian soldiers, marching as to war ...'

The soaring shout blew into her on a gust of wind. Her knees began to knock. She moaned—so quietly that the noise never got out of her.

'With the Cross of Jesus ...' He lowered the spade and made a parody of a cross with his arm, and his dark glee rippled on the increasing violence of the night.

10

She was on her knees, facing back into the barn. Carefully she lowered her legs out of the door. He had looked straight at her—raised his head up and back—but he hadn't seen her. It had taken her a minute or two before she realised. He had actually slushed his way round the corner of the barn and disappeared from sight before she knew he hadn't seen her. Her fingers gripped the ledge at the bottom of the door as her arms gradually took the strain of her body.

'Onward Christian soldiers ...' The words emptily banged about her head with their whiff of chalk and school. The rain was in her hair, running about her ears. Her heart was knocking quietly, unevenly. The night was full of noise, but she couldn't hear him. Was he opening the door now? She let go of the ledge and crashed to the ground. She veered upwards, spluttering and shaking, waist-deep in snow, and pushed herself out until the snow was only ankle deep on the wind-swept crown of the field.

She looked back at the barn but couldn't see him. He was there, of course. It seemed as though he sat on her shoulder, some misshapen hump, a claw raised against the nape of her neck. She was panting hard, though she hadn't been hurt in the fall, for the snow had feathered her crashing body.

She could move down by the farmhouse to the road, but she didn't want to go back, didn't want to go towards him. Too terrible. She would take a sweep round the mountain and drop on to the road where the Owd Bett's inn nestled.

She turned to look at the monstrous darkness that was Rake Top. She couldn't see its summit, but she could feel its coldness, the rain clouds hurtling down from the icy Pennine heights.

The mountain was a killer too, but she knew its ways: even under snow she could read it, and if she was careful it would release her unharmed. She began to move through the slush, away from the buildings, into the grey, washing moorland. The hawthorn, whose rib-cage had been in many of her dreams, beckoned her with soughing movements. She looked back again but she could see nothing.

The ankle she had injured in the car crash dragged a little, but still she walked swiftly, becoming more confident as the farm grew smaller and the mountain steeper. She was ploughing into thicker snow. She had reached the stone boundary wall, which he had climbed with the aid of his spade. Where was he?

Her fingers, already numb, dug between the stones at the top of the wall as she heaved herself up, straddling the top. She could see a thin mean beam of light below her, near the barn, flickering over the tracks he had made as he came off the moor. Soon it would search out her trail. She knew he would follow it, hunt her down, and she felt the icy beginnings of a terrible anger. It was then that she decided to kill him. She stayed, straddled across the wall, and schemed how she would bring about his death. The light had flickered into a wider arc now and rippled over the hole she had made in the snow as she crashed from the upper storey door. It picked out her trail. The light moved slowly. He was following her.

Turning her jacket collar up about her frozen face, she dropped quietly on to the other side of the wall and began to track to the left. If he were careful in following her footsteps he would be safe, she thought, safe for a while.

146

A vicious gust of wind tugged at her feet, and she bent over, using a hand to reach out and grasp a boulder to pull herself up with more quickly. Soon the mountain would shelve again into a small valley where a straggling line of aspens grew. At the north end old quarry workings had left a scree, and just beyond sight there was a cliff whose small but evil face led to the upper flanks of Rake Top. She was moving steadily now—not quickly, but economically. For the first time since she had been trapped at The Bield she felt a small surge of self-confidence. This slippery, slushing ground—this was her country. Her father, lifting her on to his shoulders when she was too tired to walk any further ... her hands in his hair, her legs scissoring his neck, the mountain swaying in her vision, scudding clouds splitting their sides with winter suns, summer suns, the feel of stinging squalls covering her face in their icy wetness, her father carrying her weight easily. Their country. Together they whistled lusty, crusty songs from the thirties. His songs.

Her feet slithered from under her and she fell flat on her face. Her cry was cut off and she hauled herself up again. Slush was running down her neck. She lifted her head to the mountain—an acknowledgment of its destructive force, a force she was taking to herself, investing herself with the primordial element of its being.

The rain blinded her. She bent her head again, protecting herself from the howling night. She was moving now, creeping along the treacherous surfaces, feeling stones rattle, snow move. Everything was charged with the growing feeling of her elation, so her world glittered darkly, beadily, back at her. Her elation grew and grew. 'I'm going to kill you, Leo. Oh Leo, you are dead!' The exuberant shout was whooshed off her lips and tossed high into the black boiling sky.

She turned to look back, suddenly anxious. Yes, there was the light, swinging drunkenly some way behind her. All at once it dipped. Had he fallen? Was he down?

'Come on,' she crooned. 'Come on, my dear. Follow me. Come on.' Momentarily blinded with hate, she stood still, steadying herself against a slab of upright granite. She began to move again, into deeper snow, and then she was on her hands and knees, catching at the hidden turf and rock. Snow burned into her hands. Gaining flatter land, she was on her feet again, and she could see the curve of the mountain's shoulder in front of her raking viciously down to the valley below.

'They say it's a she-devil at heart.' Her father's voice came back through the years. 'And the old stone ring, you know, by the north col—they say she took up male blood there. Soaked it through her pores into her vitals. The old days.' 'How long? When?' 'It's just a tale. An old tale. Valley talk.' 'I've never heard no one talk about it.' 'Valley knowledge. New people. All the new people, they don't know nothing. Don't even raise their eyes above their bellies. Don't know Rake Top's here. Let alone feel th'old bitch's bones. Not proper alive, them people. Not like us. We was always here. Through all the generations. Not like your mam. She's from Manchester ways. City folk.' He pulled down his hat and hunched his shoulders. She had somehow sensed his loneliness and reached out for his hand. He had stooped and picked her a harebell, looking sadly at its gently filmed blue: 'Not clean any more. Even up here. The whole bloody world's mucky!'

But it was clean tonight, she thought—shockingly, icily washed with sweep after sweep of rain and the snow sliding and moaning. She picked her way across a gushing stream which had formed near the summit and found a sheep track to carry its weight downwards. She raised a rain-steaming head. The whole mountain is dissolving, she thought; and wicked elation bubbled up in her.

As she moved briskly down on the bare wind-swept shoulder of Rake Top, the wind lifted her jacket in a sudden frill. She found her feet, dancing. 'I'll get you,

Leo. I'll have your hide.' She turned to look back. There was no light. The mountain was grey-black in its sloughing coat of snow. The moon broke through, lividly streaking the landscape. She looked upwards and saw its face go away, slammed behind the cloud. She gazed down the mountainside. He was gone too. Disappointment began to blow up a deadening void in her consciousness. He wasn't there. Gone. Then she saw the light again, thin and mean and swinging. Leo was coming after all.

She was on the rib of the mountain now, dropping into a small valley. Ahead were the skeletal heads of the aspen trees. It was getting quieter, the snow deeper, as she worked her way further into the bottom land. Soon the noise of storm water reached her, and in the distance she could see a bleak glimmer of the usually placid stream which threaded the valley. To her left was the shadowed remains of an old bleach works, its three eyeless windows overlooking her tracks. She felt a hissing murmuring within the ruined face and there was a prickling at the nape of her neck. She knew that all that lay beyond the windows was colonies of brambles, but her mind was filled with apprehensions. 'What am I doing here?' she muttered in sudden fright.

Sloping by the windows, she increased her speed as the terrain shelved in a gentle incline to the belt of trees. She needn't look back. He would, of course, be following. She remembered him that morning when he came to wake her, aware again of the affection in his glance. What had happened? What had become of them both? His wife. The indent of her toe clearly showing through the shroud, and Dermott, too, both as frigid as the uneaten broccoli in its white tureen in the dining-room of The Bield. Real? She began to shake under the pressure of images, so that for a moment she thought she too, like the snow, would disintegrate. The dead hair—so abundant, so luxurious. She was crying when she reached the belt of aspens.

She had always loved this small straggle of trees whose bark gleamed like snake-skin and whose branches moved upwards almost without bending. She hadn't been able to climb them as she had climbed the gnarled oaks, but their elegance had threaded her consciousness like needles of light. She had never been able to say to anyone, 'These aspens are beautiful.' So she had always hugged the knowledge to her, and now she laid a trail for Leo to follow through them, not because it was necessary, but because she wanted him to see her treasure before she killed him. She began to hum softly to herself as she skirted a small hollow hidden beneath the snow. Her elation was growing again.

Breaking through the trees, she began to move upwards. Soon she was slowed down by the knowledge that under the thinning snow was loose scree. She picked her way east across the face of Rake Top, and the wind began to roar in her ears as she broke shelter. She paused to gain her breath. He was in her woods now. She could see the flicker-flicker of his little light. Did he still think he was the hunter? She was amused. Suddenly she was slipping as the scree beneath her shifted. She thrust out her arms to stop the fall. She rolled and sat up, slush dropping off her. The mountain might have her, the mountain might have her yet. Her elation was gone. She gritted her teeth and pulled herself up.

She would accept it all, winning or losing, because she must. One day she would lose, anyway. Death was always waiting. She was ever more cautious as she crossed the scree. Already she could see the cliff face in front of her. She felt cold through to the centre of her bones.

The moon was out again. She stood still, shocked. The surrounding cliff-face gleamed viciously. Small cataracts of water surged out of its crevices. She had climbed it, yes, many times in the heat of summer, the stirrings of sulphur sometimes kicking up even though she was far from the valley factories and their chimneys. But could she climb it now? Slush riding off its boulders, night oozing among loose stones? Numbed fingers, frozen feet? Freezing wind? She must have been mad to plan such a route. Snow fell suddenly from the upper reaches of granite and stung about her ears. Her legs had been burning for some time now; the wet cloth of her trousers must have rubbed her skin raw. As she looked back, she saw that he had already reached the bottom of the loose scree. He was gaining on her, she realised. Breaking a trail was slower work than following it.

There was no way out, and she turned back to the cliff. She must climb the face.

She moved off to the left, approaching the cliff obliquely, her head down, like a high-jumper. She only looked upwards when she was already on the face. There she measured the distance between herself and the elderberry lurching in the wind near the top. It was a long way up, but as she had begun she continued, cautious, testing the ground before her. He could just move in her footsteps, gaining on her all the time. Would he catch her before she could kill him? She was on her hands and knees, numbed fingers searching unfeelingly along ever higher ledges of granite. Slush rained on her. Her feet slithered. She heard a rumble of snow further away to her left, felt the tremor of the mountain as it tumbled. A big slide. Any fall like that near to her would take her with it. She had reached the outcrop of rock she knew marked the half-way stage, and as she sheltered momentarily in its lee, trembling, she knew the worst was before her. She moved along the wide ledge, her back to the granite, seeing his light below her as she worked her way across the face.

'Christie!' He was looking upwards, his face illuminated by sudden moonlight. He was without his glasses, she realised. Had he lost them in a tumble? He looked vulnerable without them. Those spectacles of his had taken such a hold of her imagination, she realised.

Magician's crystal balls. 'Christie!' She could hear his voice plainly now.

She ignored him, working her way onwards.

'You'll fall! You'll break your bloody neck. Christie!'

She had almost reached the crazed chimney that led to the top.

'Come down. Down! I won't hurt you!'

She laughed to herself. He was afraid. Afraid of climbing up after her. She reached the chimney. The wind squealed down it.

'Christie!'

She touched the rock, and water ran between her fingers. She was very still. 'I'm done for.' As she spoke, her knees began to tremble. She wedged herself in the cradle of icy granite and slowly began to shunt her slithery body upwards, her back and legs forming a plank-like tension between the two walls. Snow cascaded freezingly into her face, and she shook her head to free her eyes. A boot slithered from its precarious hold and she fought for her balance. Slush flew around her, as she moved upwards again. A branch of the elderberry slapped her in the face. Her fingers touched the branch, and her feet slithered away. She grabbed out wildly, swinging in space, her hand clutching the branch as she bumped into the granite. She howled.

'Christie!' His voice was faint in the drenching darkness.

She swung upwards and caught the branch with her other hand, thrusting her legs forward. As her feet found rock, she tensed her body and, rigid between the rock faces again, pulled and shunted to the top of the chimney.

Her head emerged. A down draught shook her neck, pushing her face into the ground. She hauled her body out, trembling and crying quietly. She could hear his crashings somewhere below her. He might be killed or injured here, on this short rock face. Should she wait and

152

see? Now she could hear him swearing, a low monotone threading the shrill wind. A fresh gust of rain rattled about her ears.

She considered. He was a man obsessed. He would reach her if he could. He would will himself to the top of the chimney, cursing and sliding, but relentless. He would have her. He would take her. There was such a hunger in him, such a need to finish it all.

His cursing sounded louder. How close was he to her? She felt his spirit at her back, rustling at her neck. She got up. She was still crying as she moved east across the mountain. Her trousers cut into raw thighs.

In sudden moonlight the slope glistened like an opal. It can't all be real, she thought. The world is not real. It shines and gleams like a jewelled cave and I move through it like a hurtling wind. She became aware of a surprising lightness in her head, a billowing towards drowsiness.

Shock, she thought. Was she in shock? Or just tired? They had already come some way, she and Leo, perhaps three miles.

The windscreen of the Volkswagen turned in her vision, a slow, fantastic arc of light-trapped blizzard. Had she fallen off the edge of the world then? Is that what had happened? She had even worried about the damage to the car, she remembered—about the lies she would tell David. How could all that have mattered to her?

Leo. Only Leo now. But could she kill him? She turned to look back across the slope. The wind had begun to die down. The rain was falling in a persistent stream. The mountain still occasionally gleamed hoarily, a great, white shark. She couldn't see the light from his torch, but she was confident he was behind her. The chimney must have given him trouble, but he would conquer it, he would follow her: on and on he'd come. She increased her speed. She needed time to arrange his death.

Suddenly she threw back her head and opened her

mouth, drinking in as much of the night as she could. 'This is where I belong,' she thought. 'This is, after all, my world. When he left The Bield he came into my territory. I am king here.' And the power she had felt earlier, the exultation, came to her again, and she grew stronger. Her stride lengthened, her feet skimmed the treacherous mountain. She could kill him. He had said as much. He had acknowledged it long ago.

'Magicians—people like you,' he had said. He had known all along about her, about who she was—though he hadn't put it in the portrait he had drawn of her. He had only shown David's wife, damn him.

The landscape of Rake Top was changing. Great chasms were clawed out of its belly, black-rimmed, steaming in rain, waiting. She paused. She was breathing heavily. Her hand massaged the stitch in her side. When she looked back she could see his light again, but the ascent up the chimney had delayed him. Her eye followed the line she would take. She would keep high, skirt round the small valley with its chasms, taking a half-circle by the remains of the old stone ring, along the bare rock, to the end of her journey.

But would she do it? Would she really do it?

Well, soon now she would find out: soon she would know. And so would he.

A feeling of sadness came to her. To end it all. To end it all like this. But there was no other end, was there?

She moved on, slower now, grief already touching her. His small, muscular body had been like Pan's, and like Pan he had danced on his toes. His smoked skin gleamed by the burning sack in the cellar. Past tense, past tense already. How could she love him? How could she love such a man? No, no. She didn't. It was just … she might have. Their spirits were familiar, after all. It could have been so different. That was what her grief was for: lost possibilities, lost life. If only the rain would stop. It baffled everything.

154

The ancient stones were to her right, filed small by the elements. But if you stood in their protection on a quiet summer's day you could—if you were as still as death—feel them, feel their sanctity, feel their thought coming through hundreds of years. It was frightening. She hadn't done it often. As she went by she instinctively bent a head in their direction, acknowledging all that they were.

She turned from her path, coming now to the end of her journey. Already she was tingling with horror. The moon had come out, showing the ghostly shape of the familiar landscape. She moved slowly through growing heaps of stones, her body swaying slightly, as if she were taking part in a ceremony. Coming to a halt, she surveyed the land to her right. The snow was still quite deep, as deep as she had thought it would be, and came above her ankles.

She struck out in a straight line, and then, when she saw a crouch of gorse bushes, she carefully began to execute a circle, bent low, her hand eradicating her trail as she went. It was slow work. Was she being quick enough? Would he see her at her task? She completed her detour, moving back in a straight line and still camouflaging her tracks. She stopped short, as though in the middle of nowhere, divided now from her original straight line by only ten feet of virgin snow. Dropping on her knees and spread-eagling her limbs on the snow, she lay like a broken doll.

Would he notice the disturbance in her tracks, creep round to her and take her? Or would his eyes be on her tumbled figure. Would he rush in, straight towards her? There would be no immediate way of knowing. She couldn't raise her head. Her hand moved slowly into her jacket pocket and felt the knife she had honed in Dermott's sharpener.

'Christie!' His yell was close. Her shoulders twitched convulsively. 'Christie!' She could hear his blundering. It took all her will to keep her body rigid on the snow.

'Christie. Christie, love!' The voice was very near now. She went quiet inside. The whole of her being was waiting, listening. 'Christie, love …' His voice was so familiar, so comforting. My God, was there some ghastly mistake? Had she dreamt it all, the barn, the figures? It was all unreal.

'Christie, love!' There it was again. So ordinary. So right. She raised her head. 'Leo! Oh Leo! Leo! Leo! Leo!'

And then she saw him disappear. The snow opened up and swallowed him. He was so astonished he didn't yell until he was already inside the earth. Far, far below her was a distant splash. She heard the last of him while the snow was still flung up in the air. It was so quick. She rubbed her eyes. The gash in the surface of the snow was ugly. He was gone. 'Leo. Oh Leo!' She gazed bewilderedly at his blundering tracks, at the round hole that had swallowed him into the mountain's belly.

The rain began to pelt down harder than ever She sat there a long time, oblivious of its lashing. Her eyes never left the hole. He was gone. Yes, it was true. It really was. The evidence was there before her eyes. *Leo was dead.*

Slowly she began to warm. The spurt of exultation grew. She had done it. *He was dead. She was alive.* Her time ran goldenly in front of her, wedges of fat grasses, thrusting dock leaves, heat-honed limbs of future summers. She was up again, her thrilled feet dancing through the slush—in love with it all, the rain, the darkness, the coldness, the life.

And then she was off, the ancient ring of stones behind her, the old glory hole behind her. She was off down the mountain, her head still ringing with being alive. 'Christie!' Her name penetrated the drenching night, searing through the darkness, moving forever down a minute fissure of time. 'Christie-e-e-e!'

Her movements were still as economical as ever, fitting into the mountain, part of the mountain. She laughed to herself. 'I'm alive. I'm me! I'm me. I'm alive. I'm me!'

She spoke aloud, so used now to being alone that speaking to herself, the mountain, was quite natural.

Even when she became aware that she was being followed, her exultation wasn't dimmed. Let the spirits come as they might. She was, after all, wasn't she? Christie. She was alive.

She was ready to make her final descent past The Bield but paused for whatever it was to show itself. She sensed that the dark was growing lighter, that the night was over. The dog slithered down to her. It licked at her trousers and then gazed up at her with serene amber eyes.

Together they set off, down to the wall which marked the farm boundary. The rain had stopped. The wind was up again, a raw dawn raking off the mountain. 'It's all over,' she told the dog. Her exultation was dying.

By the barn she stopped. There was still snow round the edges of the farmyard, but the centre was slush. Dermott's leather coat, thrown up by the wind, dangled from the branches of the oak by the farmhouse door. She turned and was violently sick, tears running down her face. The dog sat and waited until it was all over and when she recovered it thrust a nose into her hand. 'Just like Mick,' she murmured. 'Just like Mother's dog.'

They hurried through the slush to the tubular farmyard gate. It froze in her fingers. For the first time for hours she was becoming properly aware of her physical discomforts, the rawness of her thighs where wet cloth had sawed the skin, the burning in her injured ankle, the rubbed, bleeding feet. Wearily she hoisted herself up and over the gate. The dog squeezed its wet fur through the bars.

She took one last look at The Bield, the barn, the house, the tree with its ariel skirt of roots and the flap, flap, flapping of the coat caught up in frigid branches. Wiping the tears from her eyes, she limped off down the track to the road.

It was getting lighter all the time, with objects slowly

emerging from the gloom about to assume, as they would soon, very soon, the flat and frightening reality of steel day.

The soreness of her limbs was constantly ripping small painful holes in her mind, but she went on. She daren't stop, or she mightn't get going again. When she reached the road she didn't even look behind and about her.

But lower down she saw the Volkswagen, prim and upright, as if it had been decorously driven into a ditch. But hadn't the windscreen gone round and round in her head—a fearful, lighted, revolving blizzard? Or had fright made her vision spiral?

How she had worried about the car, the damage, what she would tell David! It seemed part of another world and even though she was now going back to that world it held no reality as yet.

Back to David.

She plodded on, down to the inn at Owd Bett's. The dawn had come, though she wasn't sure when. It had been night, and now it was day—a hard, pewter light exposing Rake Top, exposing her and the dog in iced monotones.

She saw the moorland cottage where she had lived. She was almost level with the faded green door before she realised that this time she had confronted the building without the familiar painful tightening in the stomach.

She turned back to look at Rake Top, surveying it quietly—her mountain, the mountain her father had transmitted to her. It was with love she had taken his offering, a love in which she had found her survival.

She walked on. She was slowly beginning to regain her earlier exultation. This time she had come off Rake Top and had brought some of the mountain with her. This time it was different, she knew for sure. No longer was she fast in the thickets of early youth. My God, she was on the move!

A long single row of terraced houses curved up to

reach her. 'Good morning!' she shouted to the woman collecting milk off her doorstep. The woman, worn thin like the stones in the circle on the mountain, stared at her, running knobbly hands down the flanks of her nylon overall. 'That's as maybe,' she muttered, sweeping up her milk and slamming her front door.

Quiet joy ran through Christie. It was there, wasn't it? A new life. A new beginning. She felt linked to the past, woman to woman to woman, repeating down through the ages, carrying past into future—future life, future consciousness. She, Christie, possessed magic in her body—new eyes to perceive the shapes, the shadows, the substance, the raging light of being.

Now there were houses on both sides of the road. In the distance she could see the paper boy getting off his bike as he began his climb. She heard the rumble of the early diesel train on its way to Manchester. A work's siren screamed. Soon she would be off the mountain altogether.

An early morning worker, his knap-sack over his shoulder, shouted: 'Hey, luv! Hast tha been in a fight then?' He was grinning.

She grinned back.

'Hast tha?'

'Something like that!'

'Give 'im a thick ear then? Hey! Hast tha seen thi-seln? Inside o' yon rubbish bin's nothing on it!' He gave her a sardonic salute and turned down a side street.

Christie was home. It was more than relief. It was happiness. Her fingers lightly touched her belly. She staggered slightly, drunk with life.